PATRICIA ST JOHN

I Needed a Neighbour

ISBN 978 1 84427 287 7

Scripture Union
207–209 Queensway, Bletchley, Milton Keynes, MK2 2EB, England
Email: info@scriptureunion.org.uk
Website: www.scriptureunion.org.uk

Scripture Union Australia
Locked Bag 2, Central Coast Business Centre, NSW 2252
Website: www.scriptureunion.org.au

Scripture Union USA
PO Box 987, Valley Forge, PA 19482
Website: www.scriptureunion.org

British Library Cataloguing-in-Publication Data.
A catalogue record of this book is available from the British Library.

Printed and bound in Great Britain by Creative Print and Design (Wales), Ebbw Vale

Cover design by Go Ballistic
Internal design and layout by Author and Publisher Services

& Scripture Union is an international Christian charity working with churches in more than 130 countries, providing resources to bring the good news about Jesus Christ to children, young people and families and to encourage them to develop spiritually through the Bible and prayer.

As well as our network of volunteers, staff and associates who run holidays, church-based events and school Christian groups, we produce a wide range of publications and support those who use our resources through training programmes.

I needed a neighbour

1

It was half past four on an April morning when Emma woke and looked up into a pearl blue sky flecked with rose and wondered how to face another day.

It was still blessedly cool; another hour and a half or so before the sun, like some blazing monster, would rise to scorch and wither the earth. She need not move yet, although Anne, the team leader, was already padding purposefully toward the corrugated enclosure that housed the shower. But Anne was always half an hour earlier than anyone else and half an hour too soon, so that need not worry Emma. The occupants of the other five beds scattered about on the cracked earth of the compound were fast asleep and it was quite quiet. April in England, thought Emma. At this time of the morning, the dawn chorus would be starting up. But there were no birds in this dry and thirsty land and no sign of spring.

There was something else at the back of her mind and, after a moment or two, she remembered. It was her birthday. She had only arrived from England five days previously and she had not told anyone about her birthday, nor would there be any post for another ten days when someone would be coming down from the capital. A great wave of homesickness swept over her as she remembered birthdays past; the laughing girls in the nurses' home gathering round her cake; the vicarage in Devon and the presents on the breakfast table; foam of blossom in the garden, soft rain on springing grass or great stretches of sun-kissed dandelions; her mother... she swallowed hard, wiped her eyes and gazed round at the scattered beds, the thatched hut that was far too hot to sleep in, the corrugated iron shelters that concealed the shower and the hole in the ground, and pulled herself together. Everyone said she would get used to the heat in a few days; others had and she supposed she would too. In any case, it would be better today because there would be more to do. For today the first consignment of 20,000 refugees was due to arrive at the new camp.

The others were stirring so she got up and queued for the shower. Breakfast was a hasty meal of tea, bread and bananas but this would improve when stores came down from the capital. By five-thirty, Anne was rounding up her team like an anxious goatherd and telling them not for the first time that the lorries were due to arrive before sunrise. They packed into the jeep along with four or five African orderlies and then they were off, rattling through the sleeping village, over the bridge that spanned the great dam and over the trackless drought-desert with the sunrise behind them. Stunted trees and the carcasses of dead animals were the only objects that broke the monotony of the landscape, unless you counted the strange mirages of green growth and pools of water that kept appearing on the horizon and faded as the jeep drew nearer.

A clatter and a shout made them all turn their heads in one direction. An open cattle truck, with about forty people clinging frantically to the bars or holding on to each other in the centre, careered past them. Anne gave an exclamation of indignation for the driver had no business to be driving at that speed, shaking the very bones of the sick and starving. The jeep accelerated in hot pursuit and lines of tents came into sight. The two vehicles arrived almost nose to tail and the team bundled out.

Well trained by Anne, they all knew exactly what to do. Some went into the great shelters and waited at their posts by the registration desk, the weighing machines, the medical or therapeutic centres. Anne and Emma, with a group of orderlies, hurried to the truck. As they lifted the bars at the back the travellers swarmed forward and a crowd of little children, hauntingly thin but happy to have arrived, scrambled down and started to shake hands excitedly with everyone in sight. Fathers followed to receive the packages and water pots that their wives handed down to them, and the old and the sick were helped out. Then a woman with frightened eyes handed a light bundle in a goatskin to Emma, climbed out and stood beside her, looking up imploringly into her face.

Other trucks were arriving, swerving into line, disgorging their packed human cargo. About sixteen hundred travellers would arrive that morning, but Emma was suddenly only conscious of that pathetic, flickering little life in her arms. She turned to Anne.

'It's dying,' she said. 'Shall I take it straight away?'

'Yes, hurry,' replied Anne briefly. 'Clare's over at the feeding centre and she'll have everything laid out. Tell Catherine to come in your place, and send someone up to the Red Cross Department. They might produce a doctor.'

Emma hurried. Pushing her way through the bewildered new arrivals that were by now crowding round the milk cauldrons, she reached the feeding centre where Clare was teaching the orderlies, in preparation for the expected onslaught of very sick, dehydrated children. But she broke off when she saw the baby in Emma's arms and together they acted swiftly, passing a nasal tube and starting to inject the life-giving fluid into the tiny, wizened body.

'It's cold,' said Emma desperately. 'Isn't there something to wrap it in?'

'Yes, there's a box over there with some knitted clothes and blankets. Give it to me and take what you like.'

They dressed it in a striped rainbow-hued vest and wrapped it in a multicoloured blanket. Emma carried the incongruous little bundle to the doorway where the sun shone, a startling blob of colour in the midst of those drab surroundings; brown earth, brown rags, brown bundles. But the mugs of milk were bright orange and the spears of light that pierced the palm leaf roof sparkled on specks of dust and made tiny pools of brightness on the floor. The place was beginning to fill up now with families of children who had been found to be drastically underweight. Exhausted mothers carrying babies with huge heads, swollen stomachs and stick-like limbs, slumped on the floor. Hope flickered in dark, hopeless eyes as the milk, gruel and high protein biscuits were distributed. And the day grew hotter and hotter.

Emma placed her baby in the arms of an orderly and moved from group to group, encouraging them to feed or passing catheters through the nostrils of those too weak to suck or chew. She knew not a word of the language but she tried to smile at the mute, lifted faces of the parents and a few smiled back. Some were too tired to cooperate and simply lay down on the rush mats to sleep, leaving their child, at last, to someone else's care.

The only doctor was busy elsewhere. The little families came and went on coming; the nurses and orderlies worked on and on but Emma's heart stayed with the brightly-clad, gasping little creature near the door. 'Please God, let it live,' she had cried as she handed it over, but now, moving from one starved, broken child to another, she wondered dully and rebelliously what purpose there could be in such existences. What had they to live for? Nevertheless, she hurried back whenever she could to nurse the baby in the doorway.

It was hopeless; as fast as they injected the fluid into its wasted body, just as fast it flowed away. There were no nappies and water was strictly rationed. Emma took the soaking goatskin outside and laid it in the sun. With the temperature rising to 120 degrees it would dry in a few minutes.

She was holding the baby, gazing down at it, when it opened its mouth, gave a shuddering little breath, and died. Clare came over and they examined it together but there was no doubt about it at all. They turned to the mother who sat motionless, half asleep. They made signs, stripped it of its foreign finery, and laid it in her arms. She understood at once and started to wail softly. Then she stopped, and seemed to be pleading for something, pointing to her dead child.

Clare turned to the orderly. 'Ask her what she wants,' she said gently.

'She wants white cloth to wrap her baby for burial,' explained the orderly.

Clare went to search, but there was no white cloth, not so much as a handkerchief or a petticoat. Tissues, jeans and T-shirts were the order of the day. The mother wrapped the baby in a soiled rag and went away to her tent still wailing softly.

'White cloth!' exclaimed Clare. 'That's something we must see to before tomorrow.' But Emma wasn't listening; she had turned away, seeking a place to weep.

Clare squeezed her arm. 'I know,' she said. 'I felt just like that at first. You just have to get used to it... and what sort of a life is it, anyway? Go behind those biscuit cartons and get over it and then get back to those who are going to recover.'

Emma crouched behind the cartons, trying to control herself, but was startled by the touch of a hand on her arm. Half angry at being discovered, she wiped away her tears and looked into the face of a girl, so thin and stunted that it was impossible to guess her age. On her back she carried a gargoyle-like child. She was saying something and it seemed urgent.

Emma blew her nose hard and called an orderly. 'What does she want?' she asked.

'She says she wants to help,' replied the orderly gravely.

'To help me? Tell her I thank her. Ask her what her name is.'

'Her name is Mehrit.'

'And the child on her back; is it her child?'

'No, it is her brother. They have no parents.'

'No parents? Ask her how old she is.'

'She is 14; she wants to help you.'

Fourteen. The same age as Becky, her little sister! Becky, the adored youngest of a large family; Becky, who went into ecstasies over her Valentine cards and worried so much about her weight and whether she should diet! Could there be anything in common between Becky and this grave, responsible child with the sunken, suffering, compassionate eyes?

'Tell her I thank her and I will be glad if she will
help me,' said Emma. 'Tell her she can collect up the
mugs now.'

Mehrit looked her straight in the face and smiled
before she moved off; like a sort of pledge, thought
Emma, her tears forgotten. She and Mehrit would
work together and she no longer wondered how to
get through another day. In spite of the heat and the
perspiration trickling down her neck, she was glad
she had come, glad to give and heal and comfort;
perhaps she might even help to restore to health that
caricature of a child that flopped on Mehrit's back.
She suddenly decided that this stifling, crowded
shelter was the best place in the world for a young
nurse-to-be.

But who was Mehrit and where did she come
from? What strange wind of fate had brought them
together across thousands of miles? Where was her
home and what had happened to her parents? Could
Emma ever discover her story? She did not know.
She only knew that the touch of Mehrit's hand and
the steadfast look in her eyes had been the very best
birthday present she could possibly have received.

2

Mehrit stood at the door of her home scanning the road. Away to the west the sun was setting in an angry red behind the house roofs and her small brother was wailing for his supper. She had not felt frightened till now because, after all, the queues for food distribution were often long and she had known that her parents might be away all day; but not as late as this! A small thrill of fear shot through her because anything could happen these days. Something was always happening, only you did not talk about it – hunger, thirst, disappearance, sudden death and the endless fog of secrecy; things that must not be said, words that were only whispered, things that you overheard but must never know. It had become a way of life and it was all right as long as you kept together. But today they had been apart and night was falling swiftly and her parents had not come home.

She turned back to her brother who was now roaring and beating the floor with his hands, but it was not much of a show because he was a delicate child who had little strength. There was still food to be bought in the government-held towns but it was terribly expensive and there wasn't too much of it. Yet today the news had circulated that trucks were on the road, loaded with food and heavily protected by armed forces. People would dare to come from the countryside and her father had gone to meet his brother, for he had not seen his family for a long time. It was not easy to pass from the towns to the wild country of the freedom fighters but the market was a meeting place. Her mother had gone too, to carry an extra sack.

Mehrit had wanted them all to go together, with Tekla on the mule, but it was a long expedition and Tekla tired easily. She turned to attend to him, glad of something to do that would pass the time, but she was too late for he had fallen into an exhausted sleep. She lifted him on to the bed for he would not wake now till morning, then fetched meal to make *injera*, the soft pancakes that formed their staple diet. She mixed the dough and laid a small fire on the hearth and then went to the door to look again. When she saw her parents coming up the white, moonlit road she would light it.

She gazed up into the deep blue and stars appeared above the ragged silhouette of the mountains. It was cold at night high up on the plateau and she shivered a little and turned to tuck the burnous round Tekla. It was then that she heard the running feet and knew that there was bad news.

For unless the news was important, people did not run by night in this province. They stayed indoors – and some were so weak they could no longer run anyway. Besides, there were guards in the streets and they wanted to know everybody's business. But she knew who this messenger was even before she saw him because Fikre was always dodging the guards. He was thin and fast, he always knew exactly when the moon would rise, and he always ran in the shadow of the wall. She opened the door just wide enough to let him slip through and then shut it quickly behind him. He sat down, too out of breath to speak and she waited, a hand on her heart as if she could still its wild beating. When it was a little quieter she said, 'What is it? Tell me. It's my parents, isn't it?' But her mouth was so dry that she could only whisper.

He was sitting with his head in his hands and he could only nod. After a few moments he told her, but without looking up. 'They have taken them for resettlement,' he said, so quietly that she had to stoop to hear the words. 'Many people came to the market to buy grain. There were many soldiers, many guns and armoured cars to protect the trucks. Suddenly there was screaming and confusion and shots, and people running in all directions, even spilling the grain. They were seized as they ran and pushed into the trucks at gunpoint, men and women together – many, many of them. I saw your parents crying out that they had left children at home but no one listened. The doors were slammed and the trucks roared off.'

He stopped and there was a long, long silence. Mehrit did not faint or weep. Over the years she and her people had learned patience and the art of survival. After a time she said, 'Do you know where they have gone?'

'I think they take them to the coffee plantations,' he replied. 'They say there are harvests and rain down there; there are fewer people and they are not dying of hunger. They say some have gone of their own free choice. Perhaps one day, you could go and find them.'

'They also say that there are swamps and tsetse flies and the mosquito fever,' said Mehrit dully. 'Fikre, I can't stay here alone. We have got some grain stored and a little money. I shall take Tekla to my grandparents in the village. We will go tomorrow night. It is a new moon and very dark. We shall get past the military. I know the path over the mountain.'

He looked up, alarmed. 'No, Mehrit,' he said. 'You cannot do that. If they see you travelling out of the territory they will shoot. They will not wait to ask who you are or where you are going. Besides, there is famine in the villages. They are still pouring into the shelters outside the town. If you escape the military, you will die of starvation. Come with me to my home, Mehrit. We still have food stored and my parents will look after you both.'

She shook her head slowly. At that moment death seemed a merciful release but only in the company of her own people. Her grandparents were old and very poor now, but they were flesh of her flesh and bone of her bone. Besides, she must tell them of her parents' disappearance. There was no one else to go.

She held out her hand to Fikre. She was 14 and in another year he might have taken her as his bride. She knew that her parents had talked of it and even

discussed the dowry and she had been glad. She
would rather have gone to Fikre than to anyone else.
But they would not talk of marriage any more now. It
was just a case of surviving.

He did not try to dissuade her but his dark eyes
were very sad. 'You are fortunate,' he said quietly.
'You are right; tomorrow is the new moon and it will
be very dark. Besides, my sister's husband is on
guard. I'll take you as far as the first village and be
back before dawn. After that, there is only one
mountain to cross and the patrol dare not venture so
far outside the city. You can travel by day and arrive
before nightfall.'

They sat together for a while, but at 14 grief cannot
rob you of your sleep. Mehrit leaned back against the
wall exhausted and closed her eyes. A moment later
she was breathing deeply. Fikre laid her down on the
mattress without waking her and stood looking
down at her for a moment or two. She was beautiful
and he had waited a long time for her, but now there
was no future. She would die in the village as
thousands of others had died. He sighed and went
out into the night.

Mehrit slept until morning when Tekla snuggled
up to her and woke her. At first she wondered what
was wrong, for the sun, rising over the peaks,
streamed through the little window as usual,
revealing the specks of dust, making her want to rise
and clean the house. Then she realised that her
mother was not moving round and reality hit her like
a crushing weight. It seemed easier to lie back and be

crushed than to go on, but there was still Tekla. She
got up and fetched the meal for their breakfast and lit
the handful of firewood. There was grain to be
bought in the town at a high price and Mehrit's
father, being a motor mechanic and truck driver, had
been able to buy. She knew where he kept his little
store of money and there was still a sackful of
sorghum. Only it would not last for long. They must
leave at once.

Tekla, seeing the flame, white and dull in the
sunlight, sat down cross-legged to wait for his
breakfast and asked for his mother. But he was not
distressed when she did not appear. Mehrit, ten years
his senior, would do just as well. She took him in her
lap while he ate, and explained that their mother had
gone away but that, later on in the day, they would
go and stay with Granny. He nodded happily,
finished his food and went to sit in a patch of
sunshine on the step, lifting his face to the warmth,
and playing with a bag of pebbles. Mehrit knew that
he would stay there for a long time. She started to get
ready.

She could not carry much and it was no good
leaving anything behind in the house. She knew,
because it had all happened before, that her parents
were most unlikely to come back. One day, perhaps,
she might go to them; people sometimes volunteered
to migrate down south but it was the strong young
men who were chosen, not the girls with sickly
babies on their backs.

She made a bundle of her mother's clothes; there was not much and her jewellery had been sold long ago to buy food. One long, loose dress, her *kamis*, she would take to her granny – she would wear it hitched up round her waist because she was not yet full-grown – and she would also take a shirt of her father's for the old man. The more clothes she could wear the better, for the January nights in the highlands were bitterly cold. She must carry the rest of the grain, a pot of water and some *injera* for the journey. By the end of it she would probably have to carry Tekla as well.

She rolled up the rest of the clothing and went to her neighbour next door. Manila was a kindly woman who had sometimes helped them through hard times as her husband was in government employment. She looked up and smiled as Mehrit walked in.

'Well,' she began, 'your parents were late coming home last night. Did they bring the grain?' She broke off as she noticed the girl's strained face. 'Or have they not come? What is the matter, Mehrit? Sit down, child, and tell me!'

'They have gone,' said Mehrit. She still could not weep. 'They were taken off to the resettlement areas. Fikre saw them go. They will not come back. I am taking Tekla to our grandparents in the village. I have brought you these.'

Her voice was dead and flat and she showed no emotion. It was Manila who wept and pleaded with the girl to stay. 'There is famine out there,' she cried.

'Think of the shelters outside the town! They are still streaming in from the villages. You will be two more mouths for your grandparents to feed. Stay, Mehrit! You can move in with us.'

Mehrit shook her head. 'My grandmother's home is near the river that has not dried up,' she answered. 'Maybe they are not starving yet. It is January and in the mercy of God the lesser rains may come shortly. If we die, we die, but let us at least die with our people.'

Manila got up and went to the store at the back of the room. She came back with a bag of grain, a bottle of oil and a little money. 'You can take this,' she said. 'You will have to carry the child on your back but you can sling this round your neck. Thank God we still have enough. Come and eat here at sundown before you leave, and bring your property with you. We will look after it until you return.'

Mehrit leaned against Manila for a moment or two and held her hand, the pain in her throat and chest nearly choking her. The kindness had brought the tears near to the surface, but she must not weep yet; there was still so much to do, so much to plan and to risk. Through the open doorway she could see that Tekla was becoming restless and looking round for her. She managed to say thank you, kissed Manila's hand, and left. She must spend the rest of the day cleaning the house, washing clothes and preparing for the journey.

Neighbours came in during the day to mourn her loss but they spoke softly, for these events were not meant to be known and must be quickly forgotten. Besides, they had been told that it was paradise down south where the coffee grew: fair, cool weather, rain in abundance and plentiful harvests, houses and food. Some had believed this and gone from choice. Someone suggested that Mehrit should go to the authorities and ask to be taken too, but all agreed that a girl, fragile and small in stature, with a 4-year-old boy, had no chance of acceptance. Besides, the south covered several provinces and there was no knowing whether they would ever link up. The neighbours urged her to stay, offered help and care, but her mind was made up. When the real crunch comes, she thought, your eyes are opened and you know. Living or dying, you cry out for your own. She glanced through the window where the shadows were lengthening and the sun would soon set behind the town. She was ready to go.

3

Mehrit locked up the house before sunset and carried the rest of her belongings over to Manila's, where a meal was prepared for them. When they had eaten they sat quietly, waiting for Fikre. He would come when it was quite dark, before the rising of the new moon.

He came so softly along the blackest part of the street that Mehrit jumped when he stole into the house. No one spoke. He picked up a sleepy Tekla and tied him on his back for he must walk fast. Mehrit turned to Manila and looked up at her and for a moment they held each other close. Then they slipped out into the street.

'It's all right,' whispered Fikre, 'I have seen my sister's husband and he knows. Only I may not go far with you. He says I have to return before daybreak, but by that time the track will run straight ahead.'

'With God's help we will arrive,' murmured Mehrit. She looked rather fat in her parents' clothes and her own burnous over the top of them, but at least she was warm. She carried the food and the water on her back and her money in a bag round her waist. So far so good, but she dreaded the thought of having to carry Tekla as well.

She lived on the outskirts of the town so they were soon out in the open. Fikre knew exactly where he was going and he held her arm to prevent her slipping on the rough, dry clods. Somewhere out on the hillside, his sister's husband waited with a gun to prevent anyone passing from the government territory to the hungry freedom fighter territory where the food trucks never penetrated. They walked in silence and Tekla had fallen asleep. Away on their left, the long lines of refugee shelters massed black against the western sky which still glowed faintly. Things were better now; lorries from the capital were bringing food supplies from all over a world rudely awakened to what was taking place. But the world had woken up too late, as the endless mounds in the grey graveyards testified, and Mehrit shuddered as she remembered.

The great invasion of the starving had started when the last rains had completely failed in August. The people had sown their sorghum and barley and beans in the almost dry soil, but there would be no harvest. Nor was there any harvest from the small April rainfall. The maize had rotted in the dusty earth before it germinated. They had sold or eaten their oxen and even eaten their seed and now there was no future, so they came in their thousands to the town where food supplies were still available. Even the proud tribesmen from the eastern plains came, because their livestock, their cattle and goats and camels, had perished from hunger and thirst. There was no surplus grain in those days and nothing to give them, but still they came. Mehrit had tried to blot out from her memory some of the things that she had seen, but she could not; she knew that they must remain, imprinted on her mind for ever.

She remembered those who had been told to turn round and go home again, either to die on the dusty tracks along which they had come, or leave their dead behind them as they struggled forward. She could see, in her memory, the sudden storm of too-late, blinding rain which reduced the dust tracks to mud and the gullies to torrents. The people were too weak to plough through that mud; they fell and died in the puddles. Neither could she forget, as the food supplies started to roll in, the 150 selected to live, huddled inside an enclosure, receiving rations of food and water. But outside that enclosure some three thousand stood watching; their eyes sunk deep in their sockets. Yet no one fought or panicked. They just stood and watched with the age-old patience of a downtrodden people, hushing the feeble moans of their babies, accepting the inevitable, too weak to resist.

She had seen them prowling near the town. Their hair had fallen out or become tinged with red, their skin was pale and patchy and their eyes dim. They dropped under the tiny weight of their little children, sad creatures with aged, shrivelled faces. Older children followed – caricatures of children with huge, swollen bellies and matchstick limbs. They moaned and snuffled but they did not cry. There was nothing to cry for and it took too much effort.

Some sheltered in dust-covered tents by the roadside and some in hastily constructed booths.

Others huddled in hollows behind makeshift stone walls. The nights were bitterly cold and many would die before morning. Mehrit did not know how many had died. The earth mounds seemed endless and they did not include those who had died on the way, where the vultures and hyenas waited, also hungry, because those people still living were too weak to do more than scratch the surface of the cracked earth.

Yes, the food was coming now, but many from the country areas were too scared to come and fetch it, afraid of never returning. So many had been packed into lorries, like her parents, and taken away at gunpoint. She thought her uncle had probably been taken too for he was young and strong. Perhaps there was nobody left but the old, hungry grandparents. She hitched up her bundle and plodded on.

'Come faster,' whispered Fikre, squeezing her arm. 'The new moon is about to rise.' She tried to hurry though it was almost pitch-dark, but Fikre seemed to have cat's eyes and to know even the smallest tracks. Suddenly he stopped. 'Now,' he breathed, 'just walk quietly ahead.'

The form of a guard loomed black against an almost black sky. Fikre darted to his side and exchanged a few words. Then he was back, urging her forward. 'It's all right,' he whispered, 'but we must hurry. I have to be back before daylight.'

They hurried on in silence and then the new moon rose over the mountain peaks. It was a clear, cold night and the stars shone brilliantly. They were skirting the side of a deep ravine and Fikre stopped and lit a lantern. 'We are safe now in fighter territory,' he said. 'The military will not come here; now you can walk a little slower.' It was good to see that little light flickering on the rough track. Mehrit breathed more quietly and her heartbeat stopped galloping. Then Fikre started to talk.

'I wish I could come with you, Mehrit,' he said, 'but that would be just one more mouth to feed and besides, I have another year at school and there is all our future to think of. I will finish my studies and then, one night, I will slip out and join the fighters in the mountains, as you have done. Only a few months and I will come and look for you. By then, please God, the rains will have fallen and we will buy a plot of our own and an ox and a plough and I will teach in one of the new schools and Tekla will learn. Life will be good again one day, Mehrit. We will wait and hope.'

Her face burned in the dark for this was not the way that it should have been done. Parents arranged marriages and she had been brought up to respect the traditions. Then she remembered that there were no parents any longer, only herself and Fikre and Tekla in the vast limbo of silence and starlit darkness, broken only by the occasional cackle of a hyena or the cry of a night bird. There was no place here for formalities and traditions; just each other. She tightened her grip on his arm and ceased to feel afraid.

'I will wait for you,' she said. 'But what if we have to go west? Many are even going over the border. How will I ever find you again?'

'One day the rain will fall,' he replied. 'One day the living will come back to the land. One day the hills will be green again and the harvests will be gathered. I will keep watch on your village and God will not forsake us.'

She thought of her parents and their anguish, of the starving in the shelters, and opened her mouth to say that God had already forsaken them; but she swallowed back her words for Fikre was a devout believer and under instruction from a well-known priest. Besides, he had not yet suffered as she had suffered.

They had reached the end of the deep ravine. He stopped and lifted Tekla, fast asleep, off his back and tied him, in his goatskin, on to Mehrit's; then he helped her rearrange the grain and the clothing and the water bottle onto her shoulder or round her waist. She staggered a little under the weight but righted herself. Then he handed her a second lantern and lit it. She lifted it and saw that the path seemed to run smooth and downhill ahead of her.

'I must go back,' he said, 'or I shall never reach the city before daybreak and they will shoot if they see me. I must run all the way. Your path is straight ahead now. God go with you. You will get there before nightfall.'

He stooped and kissed her hand and she saw, by the glow, that his eyes glistened with tears. But he

turned away quickly, before she could even whisper
her thanks, and she stood watching the tiny bobbing
light receding rapidly for he was running fast. She
watched until she could see it no longer, then she
turned to the enormous loneliness of the night.

She struggled on for a time but she knew that she
could not carry Tekla for long. The combined weight
of child, water and grain was far too heavy for her.
Tekla would have to walk as soon as first light
dawned and that would slow them up a lot. She had
come out from the shadow of the mountain onto a
sloping plateau and after a while she sat down on a
rock to rest, drank a little water and looked up into
the huge night sky. The stars burned fiercely and
brilliantly and it was not as dark as she had thought.
Half asleep, her memory strayed back over the past
day, the darkest, worst day of her life. And yet... she
remembered Manila's kindness, the little gifts that
the neighbours had brought, Tekla's tight trusting
arms round her neck and Fikre's steady courage and
love. She suddenly knew, quite clearly, that she
would never want to marry anyone else and he had
promised to come for her. Perhaps it was not quite as
dark as she had imagined; the blacker the night, the
brighter the stars. She pulled Tekla round into her
arms, stretched out in the shelter of the rock, and fell
asleep.

She woke quite soon, partly because of the cold
and partly because of the light. Her eyes, heavy with
sleep, were almost dazzled by the blazing east. All
around her those strangely carved volcanic peaks

and cliffs, gashed by great gorges and riverbeds, confronted the sunrise, red sandstone and black basalt gleaming in that tremendous brightness. But ahead of her the high plateau sloped gently down toward undulating, flat-topped hills and valleys that should have been green but which now lay fold upon fold of grey dust and baked clod.

She turned from the wild scene to the immediate problems of the day ahead. Tekla must walk, at least for a time, for she could not carry him for long. She woke him and gave him a drink of water and a roll of *injera*. But he was sleepy, fretful and cold and in no mood to exert himself. In the end she picked up her bundles and walked away and he followed, protesting. She took no notice, just trudged on, and he trotted behind her, sniffing and crying, because he had no choice. He did not wish to stay alone in that vast, strange glory.

The sun rose higher and the day became hotter, but the mountain air was still clear and cool and the track still sloped downwards in a series of terraces. They passed scattered homesteads and small villages where, in years gone by, they could have rested and been welcome. But the villages were deserted, the fields dust and stubble. Only the endless rows of mounds in the cemeteries, and the occasional skeletons of goats and cattle, told the story.

Mehrit knew the way; she had been here many times as a little child, when the savannah bushes were in leaf and the rivers full of water, when the hillsides were green with crops, and doves and

bright lovebirds made song in the eucalyptus trees.
Once they had to cross a dry riverbed, where great
trees lay uprooted by floods; here there were small
islands of green, nourished from some deep,
untapped spring. So they rested and drank and ate
some more *injera*.

'We shall soon be there,' said Mehrit. 'You are a
man. You can walk a little further.'

The hillside beyond rose steeply. Tekla stuck out
his lower lip. 'Carry me,' he whined. 'My legs are too
tired.'

'No,' replied Mehrit. 'You must climb the hill
alone. When we get to the top, I will carry you.'

The sun was beginning to decline toward the west
and darkness would come early. All day long the fear
in Mehrit's heart had been growing, for they had met
no one – every village had been deserted; every
riverbed dry. Supposing her grandmother had gone!
Supposing they arrived to find an empty village and
a graveyard, far extended! They could only go on
now and see. Fighting her panic, she pushed on up
the hill, stumbling on the loose stones, dragging
Tekla, trying to reason away this nightmare. Her
grandmother lived near to a river that had never
dried up, a river that flowed from far heights where
snow lay and great forests grew. Surely they would
still be there!

At the top of the hill she tied Tekla on her back and
he promptly fell asleep, a dead weight on her already
exhausted body. It was almost sunset when she

climbed the last grey incline and looked down on the village with bated breath.

The homesteads still stood. The fields were baked hard but there were tiny green patches round the huts and threads of smoke rising into the still evening air. Far down in the valley the sunken river still gleamed. She had some way to go yet, but here, in this valley, were living people. Perhaps they would help her. She staggered on to the first thorny enclosure, and there were women lighting little fires in the dusty earth, cooking their evening meal; thin, hollow-eyed women with quiet hollow-eyed children, but they were kind. Some were coming up from the river two miles distant with goatskins of water; some were coming from the hills with handfuls of roots, dry seeds or grass. They listened to her story, sorry but unsurprised.

'Most of our men have gone to the mountains,' they said. 'Many, too, have been taken like your parents. Your grandparents are still alive. One of our sons will carry the child down the hill for you. It is not far.'

The sun disappeared behind the peaks and darkness fell swiftly. They reached the next cluster of huts in the last twilight and her grandparents came running out as she called their names. She did not notice that their land was empty and their faces gaunt. She only felt their arms round her and knew that she had reached home.

Then, for the first time, Mehrit wept.

4

Tesfai and Muna sat very close together on the ground. Others sat round them but nobody spoke because there was nothing to say. It was mid-afternoon and they had sat for a long time when the despairing silence was broken by the sound of a helicopter landing on the airstrip nearby. They watched dully, scarcely registering, for they had no thought or interest for anything just then, except for the little homes and families they had left, probably for ever.

Armed soldiers with cocked rifles stood to attention as the door of the helicopter opened and the passengers tumbled out. Then the spectators stared in real earnest, shading their eyes from the glare, for surely no helicopter had ever held so many passengers before, and these people were scared and sick. Men supported women and a few children, who wept and trembled, and some vomited as they landed. Some looked round wildly as though to flee but, seeing the guns, fell into line and straggled over toward the group on the ground, and squatted or lay down beside them.

'Food and water,' cried one, and the cry was taken up by the crowd all over the field for the sun was hot, even in January, and there was no shade.

A guard stepped forward and a truck rolled up behind him. As the back fell open, the crowd saw that it was loaded with blankets and two white men appeared with cameras and started to take photographs. The guard addressed the people.

'You will receive food and water in another area,' he told them, 'and there you will spend the night. But every one of you will receive a blanket so that you can sleep in comfort. When you have your blanket, line up and mount the trucks that are waiting behind you. Do not be afraid; you will be well looked after.'

Muna hesitated and looked at Tesfai but she saw no spark of hope in his face. It was expressionless and set and his eyes were dull with misery; having received his blanket he turned with the others. She realised then that her wild hope of escape was impossible for they were ringed by guns; so she walked with him toward the trucks that were waiting to carry them even further from Mehrit and little Tekla. 'Enough, enough!' cried the travellers as more and more people were shoved in with rifle butts while those at the back were crushed against the bars. It was difficult to breathe but, mercifully, they were open trucks. The shadows were lengthening and the air was cooler as they rattled away to their unknown destination.

They had not far to go. The trucks stopped on the high exposed plateau not far from the airstrip. Once again they were ringed by guns and huddled together, and once again they cried for food and water, for permission to leave the enclosure and relieve themselves. And the answer came back loud and clear, 'No one is forced to stay. If you wish to leave come over here and give up your blanket.'

There was a forward surge as people crowded to the spot and flung down their blankets. Many had been brought down from the north and would have nowhere to go that night but they would get home somehow. Tesfai smiled at his wife and Muna felt almost giddy with joy. They were only a few hours walk from the city; long before morning they would be back with Mehrit and Tekla.

But what was happening? The joyful rush had ceased. Those in front were arguing, pleading, weeping. A man cried out and fell back as he was prodded sharply in the chest with a rifle butt. Once again, the guns were closing in on them and the ring of armed guards stood out black in the waning light. That sudden flicker of hope died out, settling back into the silence of despair as the crowd realised that it had all been a cruel joke.

The sun had disappeared behind the western peaks and the sky above them was streaked with fire, like the judgement of God, thought Muna. To the east the land fell away for nearly seven thousand feet in rocky escarpments to the shadowed desert. Muna gazed out unseeing, hardly conscious of her physical needs, numbed by her disappointment.

Then a little sound jerked her to consciousness and she turned to look. A girl lay next to her panting with pain, a girl not much older than Mehrit, with the last light reflected in her terrified eyes. A young man bent over her, holding her clumsily, and he too was terrified.

Muna did not need to be told what was the matter. She knew at once and was instantly wholly involved; for to her empty, aching heart this girl was Mehrit – Mehrit who should have married Fikre in a year's time – and the baby, struggling its way into life, was her own grandchild. Confused by weariness and sorrow, she turned quickly to the young man.

'How long?' she asked.

He shrugged his shoulders. 'The pain has just started,' he said. 'She is young and little; I think it will be a long time.'

The girl, sensing the touch of a mother, turned and clung to her. It was now dark and bitterly cold, the guards huddled under their cloaks, guns poised, alert to every movement. The stars blazed out and the darkness seemed eternal, but to Muna there were periods of relief for she was living in the girl who was Mehrit and, as the night wore on, the pains subsided and the girl dozed, exhausted, in her arms.

Dawn broke slowly, over the desert, over the rim of the eastern sea and over the dull, hopeless faces of the captives. The air should have been fresh and invigorating but no one had been allowed to leave the enclosure and it stank. The children woke with dry lips and cried for water but the rest waited, silent and shivering, heads sunk on chests, for the sun to rise. And soon it came, low and glorious on the horizon, but bringing no hope for the new day. The girl woke in pain and screamed with a sharp contraction. But it passed off and she sank back and closed her eyes. Then there was a sudden stir among the guards and the people were ordered to queue up for bread and water. Stiffly they rose to their feet and the girl came too, supported by her husband and Muna. She drank but slipped the bread under her *kamis*.

'Stay in line,' the order rang out as the trucks rattled up and, once again, they were herded aboard, jammed together. Then suddenly their fears broke out into a cry of anguish as they saw what was ahead of them. They were travelling toward the airstrip and two jets stood waiting, doors ajar. The trucks stopped; the guards stood to attention; the people were herded like cattle on to the planes, on and on and on. The first lot were packed against the cockpit, the second lot were told to suspend themselves from bars at the side and, into the central space, more and more were crammed. Women screamed that their children were being crushed but still more came, hit with sticks if they protested. Only when some three hundred were standing in a solid mass were the doors slammed on them, and the plane took off for the south.

The flight lasted an hour and it was a nightmare ride. The air conditioning system was not working and people vomited freely or fainted. The girl, still supported by Muna and her husband, cried out as the contractions grew more frequent and her face turned grey. Suddenly she gave a great scream and would have fallen on the floor had there been any room to do so. Muna knew that, somewhere under the feet of the crowd, the little new life lay. She knew too that somehow she must rescue it, for once the doors were opened and the rush started, it would immediately be trampled and crushed.

Somehow, somehow! 'Lift me up,' cried Muna and her husband did so. She was a small woman but as others pressed back, it just made enough room. The young husband squatted and lifted the baby and Muna did what was necessary to detach the baby. The girl slumped down but the child was healthy. It opened its mouth and yelled and Muna experienced a moment of triumph. It was Mehrit's baby and it must live.

The plane landed and the doors were opened. Great draughts of fresh, mountain air blew in. The people, dizzy and sick, struggled forward and Muna held the baby high above her head. But the mother, and one or two others, lay still under the feet of the crowd and were carried away on covered stretchers.

Outside, the travellers were marched between rows of soldiers to waiting buses. Seventy-four sank into seats while another 74 stood. Later, they would change places. The young husband clung to Tesfai, weeping, and seemed unwilling even to look at the tiny girl in Muna's arms. Muna had tried to wipe it clean and had wrapped it in a piece of material torn from her own skirt. She looked round, fingered the cross that hung around her neck and prayed to the God who seemed to have deserted her.

The bus started up on its southward journey, leaving the great capital behind them. Two seats ahead of them sat a young couple, the girl staring straight in front of her with anguished eyes. Muna leaned forward. 'Where do you come from?' she asked.

'I was taken in the marketplace with you,' said the girl listlessly. She did not even look at Muna; she just continued to stare in front of her.

'You had children?' Muna probed gently.

'One baby; it was with my mother when we were taken.' The girl turned away as though she did not wish to talk. Suddenly she broke down and her tears flowed freely.

Muna leaned right over and placed the dirty little bundle on her lap. She stopped crying, stared at it as though she thought she was dreaming, and then lifted it to her breast.

5

Mehrit and Tekla lay asleep covered by a skin and their grandparents squatted beside them, mourning their daughter and trying to decide what to do.

'They must go back,' said the grandfather. He was an old man with a bald head and stick-like legs. He was a clever farmer. But he had sold his ox to buy the last store of grain and he knew that the end was not far off.

'Go back to what?' asked the grandmother. 'They cannot live alone.'

'There is food in the town and the neighbours are kind. If they stay here they will die. We cannot feed them.'

'They won't stay here. Didn't you tell me that the village was leaving? That they were meeting tomorrow to talk about travelling west? Let them travel with us and somewhere, further on, we will make a new home together.'

He glanced at her, unwilling to put his thoughts into words. He had thought that she would have known. 'We are old,' he said gently. 'How can we travel so fast and so far? There are still small stores of corn in the village and we can still reach the river. I think the old will stay.'

Grandmother shook her head. 'The children are strangers and they cannot eat from the village grain store. I am still strong and we will follow the trail to the camps. Let us all go together.'

He straightened his bent old back and smiled at her. 'If that is your wish, then we will go,' he said; for, although she was old and almost toothless, he still loved her very much. Out west it was said that there was food, but there was also war and sniping on the roads. Ah well! With drought and famine in the village there was little to lose, especially now that his daughter had been taken. Then his gaze rested on the sleeping children and he checked his tired thoughts. For their sakes, they must still live for a time and be strong. He was a peasant and he knew that the old stalks wither and die only that the seed may be scattered and grow; but they die gracefully, with dignity and without protest. Indeed, he knew there was even beauty in the last golden leaves, but nothing mattered except the new sprouting. He and his wife lay down together on the rope bed and slept peacefully, their minds made up.

The children woke refreshed and hungry. Mehrit took the water pot and went to the river in the deep ravine which had still not dried up. It was a good two hours' walk, scrambling down over shard and rock, but other women and children went with her and the mountain air was still fresh and cool. Because of the ravine into which the high snows trickled, their village had not perished like other villages. They had not been able to plough or sow, but they had been able to cultivate sorghum in the shade of their houses, toiling to and fro to sprinkle it with water.

But now the great twig-woven vats were nearly empty and there would be no harvest for it was five years since the rains had fallen. Even if the small rains came in February they could not survive until the crops ripened. Mehrit and Tekla had arrived just in time. The official permission had been given to leave and, that very morning, a meeting had been called and everyone in the village would attend.

Mehrit climbed back to the house to find her grandmother crouched over a small fire making *injera* with some of the sorghum that the girl had brought from the town, and her soldier son lay on the mud ledge beside her. He had come from the rebel forces in the mountain strongholds and had walked all night. But he sat up when he saw his niece and greeted her courteously. Tekla climbed into his lap and gazed almost worshipfully at his gun.

Grandmother blew out the fire, for every scrap of firewood was precious, and divided the *injera* carefully between them, keeping the smallest portion for herself. As they ate, they talked. Her son, Gabre, had come to organise the journey and guide them on their way to the first rest camp, for there were few young men left in the villages. He was tall and strong but the bones of his face stuck out sharply and he was very thin. His dark eyes flashed with anger when he heard what had happened to his sister and her husband, but he tried to comfort the children. 'All is not lost, little ones,' he said. 'Some have escaped over the border and returned. You too must escape over the border and, who knows? Someday, somewhere,

you may meet again.' Then he added a quick aside,
'They were fools to go to the distribution. Nobody
young and strong and in their senses goes there any
more. He should have sent the children. They
wouldn't have taken them.'

There was a stir in the little village. People were
coming from the houses, mostly the old and the
women and children. They were a haggard lot and
the children were quiet and listless. Some had bald
patches in their hair and many hung their heads, for
their eyes were inflamed and sensitive to light. But
they all came, pouring from the round stone huts, to
gather in front of the little church where the priest
was ringing a cracked bell.

It was the priest who addressed them first, a thin
old man who leaned on his stick. He told them what
they already knew, that they could no longer stave
off the famine and wait for the rains; the official
paper had come and they must pack up what
possessions they could carry and set off all together.
They could turn east to the government-held towns,
which were nearer and where food was available, or
they could start on the long march west to a more
uncertain food supply. They must decide.

There was no hesitation in their choice. The
western road might be long and dangerous, but to
the east, people disappeared and parents were
bundled into lorries and children were left behind.
They would go west. The women and older men
would carry the little ones and the older children
would carry the bundles and they would start just

before sunset. Gabre then took over and explained that it was better to travel by night. They were highland dwellers, unused to the lowland heat and, in any case, the roads were not safe by day because the enemy troops sent planes that swooped to shoot down columns of travellers. Many had died, he told them – men, women and children. But he had come to guide them. He knew the way over the mountains and it was not too far to the first rest camp.

There was dead silence as some families turned to their own old parents and grandparents already weakened by hunger and rigorous self-denial, for it was always the children who must live. Some had tottered weakly, some leaned on sticks. But there was still some grain in the village and a small store of seed, and surely the rains would come soon. Some who could not make the long journey could still walk to the water. Mehrit leaned against her grandmother.

'Tekla and I will stay with you,' she whispered. 'We cannot leave you or go alone. We will draw water for you.'

'Your grandfather and I are coming,' replied the old woman, with great spirit. 'God will give us the strength. We will stay together.'

It was a sad, sad sunset. Everyone collected in front of the church carrying a blanket, a mat, a cooking pot and a water pot and together they ate and drank, so quietly that the meal seemed almost sacramental. Each had a small store of grain for the journey and, as they journeyed west, they might find edible roots and grasses. All that could be gathered in the way of food or firewood had been left behind for the few old people who stood uncomplaining and unprotesting, for they had lived through famines before and they knew. Their children embraced them weeping, the priest blessed them, and the straggling convoy set off. When Mehrit turned at the bottom of the hill, the last rays of sun still shone on them, standing desolate, waving farewell.

And certainly the trail they followed that night through the hills was not for the very old or the very young. They kept their eyes on Gabre's bobbing lantern and the new moon gave a little light, but many of them suffered from night blindness and stumbled on the rocks or slid on the shale.

They rested in the daytime, sheltering under rocks, drawing water where they might from rivers that had almost dried up, where the pools were clouded and muddy. The boys collected firewood to cook the rapidly diminishing supplies of sorghum. Other groups of migrants joined them from other villages, but no one talked much or exchanged news and the children soon ceased to play or chatter. Sometimes two would start a conversation but soon they would seem to fall asleep in the middle of a sentence. Yet when evening came, they would rise up doggedly and set off along the trail.

Mehrit's heart sank whenever she looked at Tekla. He seemed fatter than before but it was not a healthy fatness. His stomach appeared to be swelling up but his eyes were sunk deep into his old-looking, lean little face. Gabre usually carried him and when they stopped for rest he would nestle down in his grandmother's lap and whine for food. Then Granny would take a few sticks and light a tiny fire. She would put a few drops of water in the pot and place it on the stones and rock Tekla to and fro. 'While the food heats we will sing the song of the cooking pot,' she would say, and she would sing and talk of days gone by when the grass was green and the oxen drew the plough; when they harvested the maize and the sorghum and the bees swarmed and the birds sang; when they brewed the beer and laughed and danced... in a very short time Tekla's eyes would close and he would fall into deep, exhausted sleep; and he never knew that there was no food in the cooking pot.

Yet the first to go was not a hunger victim, for as they skirted small towns they were given enough food to keep them alive but never enough to satisfy them. Selassi was a brave little boy, tramping along beside his mother, seldom complaining. Her husband had been killed in a skirmish with government troops and her baby had died. Selassi was all she had left, and for his sake she was determined to stay alive.

It was midnight and they were pressing on over the foothills, trampling the dry brushwood, sometimes whispering words of encouragement to the weary children. Suddenly there was a shrill scream and the column froze; then a rustle in the undergrowth as a snake glided away. It was a night of clouds and very dark and it took a little while to

determine who had uttered that cry, and to catch up
with Gabre and beg him to return with the lantern.
By the time he arrived, Selassi's foot was swollen and
blue and, although Gabre cut across the wound with
his knife and sucked with all his strength, it was too
late.

They could not wait. There were too many other
children in danger of death if they loitered. A man
took Selassi in his arms and they stumbled on until
the sky ahead of them flushed rose and saffron above
the rolling countryside. The man stopped and he and
the mother gazed down at Selassi's face. It had been
twisted with pain before but now it was suddenly
full of peace and alight with the dawn.

'He has gone,' said the man almost wonderingly,
and the old priest, who was nearby, held up his
golden cross.

6

'Just a couple of hours more,' said Gabre, 'and we shall be at the rest camp. Keep going.'

It was early morning and they walked slowly, remembering that small, shallow mound. Selassi's mother wept quietly, uttering the traditional cries of mourning, and the old priest walked beside her. Other mothers glanced anxiously at their children for they were low in the foothills now and the heat was increasing rapidly. There was little water left, and although the younger ones stumped along bravely, their bodies were becoming dehydrated. Gabre picked up Tekla again and they forged ahead. No one spoke but heads were lifted a little higher. At least they could see where they were going and shelter was not far off.

It was stark, arresting country that they traversed now; quartz-coloured rocks behind them, gleaming in the early sun, red-ribbed soil ahead under an azure sky. Thin, leafless forests grew on these slopes, their boughs torn off for firewood; and the day became hotter and hotter.

Then they saw it, and a feeble cheer went up – a little town nestling at the foot of a sandstone cliff with houses of black basalt or sandstone, a rock-hewn church and a green mosque. Here there must certainly be food and water. But they were not going to the town; instead they turned aside into a grove of dry, brown-leaved eucalyptus trees. An earth bank covered with bushes sloped down and Gabre turned to the disappointed crowd.

'Follow me,' he said.

He turned the corner and suddenly, they had arrived. There was a large underground shelter, invisible from the air, with raised platforms covered with plastic so that travellers could sleep out of the reach of ants and vermin. Other groups were already installed, their belongings scattered round them, and they were drinking water and eating food. Sick, exhausted children were being tended with care and kindness. To the footsore, hungry travellers it was as though they had reached paradise. They squatted in the shade of the trees and waited their turn.

Their turn came soon. They were fed and they drank and lay gratefully down to sleep, the tired children snuggled against their mothers. Only Selassi's mother lay in a corner alone, rocking herself and moaning.

They slept or lay resting all day and far on into the night; at dawn next day they were once more fed and told to fill their water bottles and collect their ration of food. 'For we shall travel till midday this morning,' said Gabre. 'Then we will rest and go on through the night.'

Grandmother rose and shook Tekla awake. Then she went to Grandfather who was lying very still. There was a big, festering sore on his foot where he had stumbled over a stone; it was covered with flies and he was breathing very rapidly. His eyes were bright and she had not seen them bright for a long time. They had been dull with hunger for many weeks.

'You have fever,' she said. 'You cannot walk. We will wait. Later on you will be able to travel.'

He shook his head urgently. 'Gabre must go with the village,' he whispered, 'and you must go with him... the children... you must take the children. I will stay here; I will not travel any more.'

She knew he was speaking the truth and she knew where her duty lay. Yet it was hard for she had lost so much. Her older daughter had been taken south and her younger daughter had married a man who lived far across the mountains and, as far as she knew, most of that village had perished in the early months of the famine. Now it was her husband whom she had married when she was 12 years old and from whom she had never been parted for a single night. One by one they had slipped away from the struggle and the hunger and the rough roads, and death seemed almost a well-known friend. Yet the parting was still hard. She had loved him when the fields were green and the earth was soft, but she had loved him much more in the empty years of drought because there was nothing left except love, and the flame burned brighter in the darkness.

Gabre stood by her side and there were tears in his eyes. 'We must go, Mother,' he said. 'They have given us our food but it will not last till the next camp

unless we start now. Here they are kind and they will
care for Father. You should come; Mehrit needs you.'

She leaned over Grandfather and gave a little
wailing cry of love and sorrow, for it was like tearing
away a part of herself. He was almost too weary to
open his eyes but he managed it. 'The children,' he
whispered. 'Go with the children.' Then he turned on
his side, closed his eyes and gave up the fight. She
knew that it would soon be over for there was
nothing left now for which he needed to live.

A kind young worker led her away. 'We will stay
with him,' he said. 'It will not be long and there is a
priest in the camp.' And this comforted the old
woman for, although she had never understood a
word of the language in which the Holy Book was
read to her in church, the priest had told her that this
world of pain and famine was not the end.
Somewhere, some day, she might see her husband
again in a land where the fields were green and
where water flowed; perhaps very soon, for she felt
as though most of her life and strength were dying
with him and she did not want to live. But for the
children's sake she must go on. She muttered the
name of Mary and every saint that she knew and set
out on the road.

For a few hours they risked travelling on a real
road, built by their own people for the transport of
their food trucks, but in the heat of the day they went
down into a little valley and rested in the rustling
shade of eucalyptus trees. Here they were safely
hidden; the pungent smell made them feel drowsy,

and most of them slept. When they woke, the shadows were lengthening and the stark colours of the burnt, rocky landscape stood out in startling shades of red and grey and black in the last rays. They lit their little fires and baked their bread while the older children explored the valley for seeds and edible roots. But they did not go far or find much, for they were weak, tired children who only wanted to rest.

It was getting dark when they set out again and although the land was still dry and desert, they were leaving the worst of the famine behind them now and the camps were closer together. The days passed in a weary pattern of resting during the days and starting again on the long, long march through the cooler nights. But some of the children with their stick-like legs walked more and more slowly and, although some of the little ones were carried, it was impossible to carry all. It was a sad sight to see a mother or father, already burdened with a baby, a toddler, blankets and a cooking pot, trying to heave along a teenage girl who could go no further.

The little convoy grew smaller as the old and the weak died. Some died of anaemia or scurvy; some developed such severe night blindness or trachoma that they could no longer see the paths and fell over the rocks into the ravines. Little children and babies died of dysentery and dehydration and the trail of earthen mounds hastily scratched from the soil by the wayside grew longer. But each time they reached the rest camps there was kindness, food and water and even elementary medical care.

They reached the west of the country where the rivers had not all dried up and, although it was only February, small showers of rain had already fallen and a thin veil of green seemed to rest like a mist on the parched land. But the population of the villages was already swelled beyond capacity by the thousands who had fled the famine, and they could not stop there. So they went on.

Crossing the rivers was a problem. The water was usually low and the men would stand in the deepest part and help the rest across, soaked and shivering, to the farther bank. There were places on the road where bridges had been built, but they dared not use them for they were prime targets for the enemy planes.

Mehrit trudged bravely along and her grandmother tottered beside her. Tekla was usually safe on Gabre's shoulders but his stomach was getting bigger and bigger and his arms and legs smaller and smaller. Suddenly one morning, on a flat stretch of rough ground, Gabre stopped and looked down, and the whole company came up to him and looked with him. A broad river flowed between banks at their feet and the trees along the verge were green.

'We will rest here and drink and wash,' said Gabre. 'Then we must cross it. The current is swift but there is a kind of ford.'

When Gabre waded in, the water rose to his chest and he was a tall man. Yet cross it they must if they were to reach the camp by next morning. One by one the men carried the children across, bidding the adults bind their belongings on their backs and hold their babies above their heads. Mehrit and Tekla were already on the far side, having been transported on Gabre's back, and he was now supporting his mother in midstream. Just then Mariam, a neighbour from the village, slipped and disappeared under the water. She surfaced, gasping and screaming, but her baby, born just before they started out, and held high above her head, had been swept away. As the tiny body reappeared and disappeared, one man after another plunged into the flood. Then there was a great shout of joy as its father caught hold of it and swam to shore.

Was it too late? The child looked blue, its eyes tight shut and its mouth wide open like a small fish. But they held it upside down and shook the water from its lungs and an older man, who had once been a medical orderly, breathed into it the kiss of life. The muddy crowd stood round motionless, fingering their crosses, while the baby's mother lay on her face, sobbing hysterically.

And then a miracle happened. The baby gave a gasp and a splutter, vomited up some river water and gasped again. Mehrit, who was close beside it, saw the pink flush under the dark skin and, as the baby opened its eyes, a great cry went up from the crowd. For the first time on that patient journey of sorrow they rejoiced together. 'The child lives! It lives!' they said to each other over and over again, and suddenly Mehrit noticed that the trees by the river were green and beautiful and there were small flowers on the bank. Even wizened little Tekla smiled and clapped his hands although he could not possibly have known what it was all about. It was as though, for one moment, life had triumphed over death and joy over sorrow.

But it was only a small break in the clouds. As they travelled on, the country was becoming more thickly populated and showing more scars of battle. Sometimes they passed through villages where every home had been demolished and where schools, clinics, and even orphanages functioned in dug-outs invisible from above. Travelling was becoming more dangerous, too, as on this bare, undulating country it was impossible to hide the ragged column of people who trudged on and on.

They travelled more by night now and the pace grew slower and slower. The nights were growing hot in the lowlands and the children, used to the high mountain air, found it very hard to go on. Grandmother talked no longer and her breath rattled as she toiled along.

The sun had risen behind them and the stumbling travellers strained their eyes to see whether the camp was in sight, but the light was too bright and they looked down at the asphalt. Rest was not far ahead and Gabre had decided to stick to the road.

At first only one or two heard it and stopped dead in their tracks, looking at each other. Then that faint humming swelled to an angry roar and parents seized up their children and rushed for cover. But there was no cover; so they flung themselves down among the thistles and shale by the side of the road, covering the small bodies with their own. And the great plane swooped almost to ground level, strafing the road with its machine guns, then tilted back into the blue, gleaming and silver in the sunrise.

For a long time no one moved. It was deathly quiet and Mehrit, lying where her grandmother had leapt on her and flung her to the ground, did not want to open her eyes to find out what had happened.

Then the weeping began and the groaning of the wounded, and those who were unhurt crawled out to see what they could do. Gabre, sheltering Tekla, had not been hit and he took command. He and two others carried the wounded to a flat place while another couple sped off to the camp to find help. The dead they laid in a shallow ditch and covered them with stones and thistles. They mourned and wept for them and the priest recited prayers, holding his gleaming cross high in the air. But Mehrit sat, rocking Tekla back and forth, seeing nothing, unmindful of food or water or heat. For she had struggled out from under her grandmother and seen the bullet wound in the back of her head; now she watched them carry the frail old body and lay it in the ditch.

So now there was no one left but Tekla, who lay shocked and listless in her arms, and her Uncle Gabre

who stood, stony-faced, looking down into that mass
grave.

7

Hundreds of miles south, Tesfai and Muna lay side by side in the frail shelter they had built from brushwood and reed matting and which they now called home. It was still dark and through the cracks in the roof they could see the blazing starlight. But the air was blessedly cool and there was still another hour before the sun would leap over the plantations like some fierce consuming animal, to sap their strength and parch their lips. Coming, as they did, from the highlands, the lowland heat was one of the worst things they had to endure.

They liked to wake early for this was their own hour. At daybreak, Tesfai would be hounded out to the coffee plantations and Muna would follow shortly after. They would probably not meet again till sunset, when they would bake their meagre rations of *injera*, swallow some water and lie down, exhausted, in their shelter to sleep, with barely a word passing between them. But in the cool of the very early morning some measure of daily strength returned to them and they would lie quietly talking, thankful for each other because so many had died. And their talk would be of the children and the possibility of escape.

Everybody talked about escape and a few had disappeared. They had gone to the latrines outside the camp and had never been seen again. The guards, however, had made sure that this would not happen any more and now no one was allowed to leave the camp outside work hours, so the enclosure stank and festered. No one could do much about it. The ground was too hard to dig, nor had they the tools. The flies grew enormous and sickness was rife. Even dead bodies lay unburied, wrapped in plastic sheets, shrivelling in the burning heat, while their relatives summoned the strength to scoop out a shallow grave. Some whispered that very soon the cholera sickness would break out and then there would be more dead bodies; many, many more dead bodies.

But the dark, early morning hour was their own and Muna lay in the shelter of her husband's arm and knew that while he lived she could go on, and that one day, the God in whom she had almost ceased to believe (she had never known much about him) would help them get back to their children. It was a kind of obsession with her and she never ceased thinking about it. Day by day she would wake with some new plan of escape only to find that it had been tried and proved impossible.

'But some have disappeared,' she whispered. 'And remember, we are not far from the border. The bus driver told us that. We know where the sun rises and sets and we only have to follow.'

'And when they follow and shoot us down, what then?' replied Tesfai patiently. His hope had almost died but he recognised and admired that fierce maternal instinct in his wife that would never give up the struggle to return to her children.

'We might try in the dark,' she whispered. 'Just before the new moon rises it is very dark indeed; or just after the new moon sets, they sleep. If we crawled out near to where the dead lie, there would be a chance. They will not sit near the dead.'

Tesfai drew her closer. 'We will talk with others,' he said. 'They might make a disturbance down the other end of the camp, so the guards would move down and leave the upper end unwatched for a few minutes. Or perhaps, after a time, they will relax their watch. As you say, the border can't be far. We could follow the path of the sun through the bush. But it's a long journey home, Muna, and we are weak.'

He was talking more to comfort her than because he had any real hope, and she knew it, but she was grateful to him. A small wind stirred the rush matting over their heads, fetid with the stench of the camp, and the darkness was paling. They lay in silence, savouring the last minutes of rest and togetherness, then Muna rose stiffly and scooped the ashes from the hole in front of the hut. She mixed the meal and water into a thick paste and lit the brushwood under the metal. They crouched in the red dawn and drank the rest of the water. Then Tesfai went to report for work and Muna set off with her plastic container to the pipeline. They were still hungry. They would eat again at night, but their supply of grain and oil had to last till the end of the month.

Muna walked slowly, partly because she was weak and the ground was rough, and partly because she was unconscious of everything except her own thoughts. Other women were converging on the water supply but Muna's feet carried her automatically and she barely noticed them. From far away, over the northern mountains, her children cried out to her, drawing her with a strength that was almost physical; Mehrit, her dark eyes drowned in distress, not knowing where to go or what to do; Tekla, sick and weak, needing her. She filled her container and walked back, her determination growing with every step. She recognised the wisdom of her husband but she wished that she could make him see that, whatever the odds, they must go. He was a loving husband and a good father, but he could not hear the voices of the children as she could.

She reached the shelter they had built on arrival and sat for a few minutes remembering. They had heard all the stories about the land of plenty to which they had been taken; there would be fruit, meat and plenty of water. But when those fetid buses had drawn to a halt and disgorged their hungry, thirsty, soiled occupants, the newcomers were faced with a small, deserted settlement whose dwellers had been forced out to make room for them. There were small areas of land which had once been cultivated but which were now dried up. There was not enough room for all, so the men were given axes and told to build their own shelters. They were given a ration of oil and grain and told to fashion their cooking pots from what they could find. The militia with their guns patrolled the whole area, escorting them in herds to the coffee plantations at dawn, and bringing them back at gunpoint in the evening through the bushes, watching them gather handfuls of firewood as they passed.

It was a land of thorny bushes and low scrub but away to the west the flatness rose to low hills with forests on their slopes. Muna had gazed at them over and over again. The scrub and thorn provided little shelter, but in the clefts of the hills and forests they could hide. Evening after evening she had watched the flaming colours as the sun set behind that undulating horizon and, in her imagination, they were fleeing through it on their way back to the children.

It was getting very hot and soon they would come and round her up with the other women to go to the plantation. She laid down her water container and crossed over to the small, crumbling hut where, amazingly, the baby still lived with its foster mother. But the girl had grown thin and her milk was beginning to dry up. She looked down hopelessly at the tiny creature at her breast and then up at Muna.

'I have come to say goodbye,' said Muna.

The girl began to cry, small jerky sobs, for she had loved Muna like her own mother. Then she dried her tears and her face became resolute.

'Many have gone,' she said quietly. 'Some have been shot but some have escaped into the bush. My husband has talked with many. This baby's father, he wants to go. He has left children at home. He wants to try. You should talk to him.'

'Tell him to come,' whispered Muna. 'Tonight we will talk. Tomorrow is the turn of the new moon.'

So that night they came and sat round the tent door, when the dusk was falling and the small fires glowed – the baby's father, two angry young men and a young couple, the woman half-crazed to get back to her family. They talked quietly, wasting no words. One was a mechanic and had fashioned a pair of wire cutters from scrap metal, for there was barbed wire round the northern end where the dead lay. As Muna had said, tomorrow was the new moon. Just before its rising, some people would start a commotion down at the southern end of the camp and by that time the wire would be cut and the escapees lying rigid by the side of the dead. When the noise started they would crawl through on their stomachs and run into the darkness in different directions, splayed out north, east and west. The guards would, no doubt, hear the crackling of the dry bush and shoot. Some would die, but some would escape. Of those who might be wounded and dragged back, they refused to think.

They crept away, each to their own shelter. Muna and Tesfai lay side by side, unable to sleep but drawing courage from each other. Tomorrow Muna must rise early, use up the rest of her grain ration and make a store of *injera*. Tomorrow they must drink well and carry only a little water. But tonight they must love and talk a little, for it might be the last night they would ever spend together. Tonight they must pray to God and Mary and all the saints to preserve them, but Muna did so half-heartedly, for where had God and Mary and all the saints been when they dragged her away from her children, when the girl had given birth to that baby in the plane, when the dead lay unburied? There was no answer to that one and she turned back to the thought of her gentle husband and leaned against him in the dark. Strange how, when all the other lights of earth burned dim or went out, the light of love seemed to burn brighter and brighter! She lay there thinking about it. Where did love come from? Was there a source? Why could neither hunger nor thirst nor misery ever quench it? Love seemed so near that night, not only in her but all around her, wooing her, covering her. She found herself smiling and at peace and she went to sleep.

Next day was blazing hot. The workers came home in the evening and ate and drank as usual, then lay down exhausted. There were very few preparations to make. They put on their dark cloaks, tied a water bottle and a roll of *injera* round their waists and Muna also tied on the flat metal pan on which to bake. Then, at the dark hour before the moon rose, they crawled on their stomachs across the earth and lay down behind the pile of dead. One by one they arrived and no one who survived ever forgot the nausea and fear of those waiting hours, nor the stealthy grinding of metal on wire.

It was after midnight. The grinding had ceased and the young mechanic lay quietly, his work done and the way open. Suddenly there was a noise of fighting and confusion and piercing shrieks from the southern end of the camp. Guards leaped from the bush, rifles cocked, and ran toward the direction of the noise, raising their lanterns, firing their guns in the air. The little waiting group wormed their way swiftly through the gap, rose to their feet and ran, north, east and west into the bush, tripping on roots, torn by thorns and low branches but running on and on toward freedom. But the patrol were no fools; they had quickly ascertained that the commotion to the south was a false alarm and came back to their posts. Somewhere out in the bush they could hear the rustling and crackling of broken branches and the angry cry of a disturbed night bird. The guards combed the bush, their guns shooting in all directions, and someone screamed and fell. Then they flung their lanterns into the thorns and a great blaze of fire lighted the whole area while they shot again and again.

Muna and Tesfai had run straight east, following the line of the margin of the camp and into the path of the night breeze which carried the flames before it. The bush was burning fiercely now and those who had run westward would hardly have a chance; but running into the wind away from that all enveloping smoke, they might make it, thought Tesfai grimly. Yet the air around them was scalding and the crackling of the flames very near. Blind with heat and swirling smoke, he stumbled on, hardly realising that Muna was lagging behind.

He only stopped when he heard her cry and fall. He ran back and helped her to rise and dragged her forward. She seemed unable to run any more but, as he turned, he had noticed something. He was no longer trampling on thorns and roots but on dry, stony earth and they had reached a clearing in the bush. He lifted her onto his back and struggled on, and as he progressed the heat became less intense and the air clearer and he knew that the fire would come no further, for he was running straight in the path of the wind. He also knew that the flames would prove an impassable barrier to their captors for hours to come. He pressed on, bowed almost double with Muna's weight until he felt that he was breathing fresh night air. Then he laid her on the ground and sprinkled her face with water. It was very dark but he could hear her breathing, and by the starlight he could see the whites of her eyes so he knew that she was looking up at him.

'Muna,' he whispered.

She spoke in little gasps. 'I cannot go on. My feet are burned and I am bleeding. You must go on without me... you must go to the children.'

But he could not leave her; he loved her more than he loved the children. He put his arm under her and felt the hot stickiness of her blood. He did not care if they pursued and shot him too for she was starting on that last journey already and he would gladly have gone with her. He wished he could see her or that there was something he could do. He tore off a strip of his shirt and tried to staunch the wound but he knew it was no good. She was quiet, her breathing rapid and her pulse racing.

'I will stay with you,' he said. 'You are my loved wife.' He took off his cloak and rolled it up to make a pillow for her and, as he did so, he realised that there was a stirring of the wind and a thinning of the darkness and a small twittering of bush birds. He closed his eyes for a moment; he could not remember feeling so weary before. When he opened them again he found that he could discern the shapes of the trees, ghostly white in the morning mist. Then he dared to look down into Muna's face; it too was ghostly-looking, her eyes were closed and the earth around her was dark-stained. Yet it was the face of peace. She might have been sleeping at his side.

He sat beside her, until the sky beyond the clearing turned opal, flecked with feathery pink clouds and then, suddenly, the east seemed to catch fire with the shot crimson, mauve and gold of dawn. He got up, took her cloak, and the *injera*, the water bottle and the pan from her waist and tied them round his own. Then he piled brushwood and stones over her and wondered what to do next. He wanted to lie down beside her and die too but he supposed he couldn't. He wished there was a priest and he thought he ought to say a prayer, but his tired brain seemed unable to remember the words.

But there were two words he did remember – the last ones she had ever spoken. He suddenly realised that there was still something to be done and that he was facing the wrong way. He must turn round and travel slightly north-west with the sun on his right shoulder.

'The children, yes, the children,' he muttered. He picked up his bundles, looked down once more at the mound and, with tears streaming down his face, set out for the border.

8

'We're nearly there,' said Gabre.

There was a pause while Tekla, such a very light burden now, summoned up the energy to lift his head and look. But his sight was no longer very good and he could only see a blur.

'Where?' he asked.

'To the camp where we are going to stop. There's food and rest there, where the trees grow by the river.'

'To stop for ever? Never go on any more?'

'Maybe; for a long time, until you get strong again.'

Tekla managed to turn and call out to Mehrit, who was just behind him, 'We're nearly there, Mehrit. And we're not going to walk any more ever again.' Then his head, which looked much too heavy for the rest of him, drooped back into Gabre's shoulder and his sunken eyes closed contentedly. It was a sharp shoulder with every bone sticking up from under the skin, but it had been his pillow for a long time and he had got used to it. Besides, he knew his good fortune; there were children, not so much older than him, still struggling along on tiny, broomstick legs. But there were not so many of them left now.

Tekla's voice was so small and weak that Mehrit scarcely heard what he said, but she knew it was something to do with that line of trees ahead, bright in the early morning sun that burned on their backs, and she managed to smile at him. Her legs seemed to be buckling under her but if this was the end, she could get there.

Sometimes, since her grandmother's death, she had wondered what was the point of going on but now there seemed to be just one overwhelming aim in life: to reach a place of shade and to lie down and rest and never to move again, so that she could take Tekla in her arms and rest him back to strength. She pressed on and the row of trees was getting nearer. She could see the crowds of people who had arrived while it was still dark, squatting patiently in the shade, waiting their turn for attention.

So many, many people! Now that she was getting closer, it looked, to her astonished gaze, like a far-stretching city of flimsy shelters – rush mats or rags balanced on uneven poles, thousands and thousands of them crowded together on the eastern bank of the river; and the banks were deep, for the great river had sunk to an all-time low. Some large pools remained and people were boring down into the sandy bed. But the water that welled up was sluggish and brown.

It was very quiet. They squatted on the outer edge of the crowd and Gabre laid Tekla in Mehrit's arms and went ahead to report the new arrivals. She looked down at his wan face, twisted to a smile, and she smiled back. Since crossing the border, the terror of further bombardment had been lifted, and she had known a strange, weary peace, but at the sight of his sharp cheekbones and sunken eyes her heart gave a lurch of fear. If Tekla died... but her imagination could go no further; she gathered him to her, stretched out on the pale earth and fell fast asleep.

***

'*Regardez!*' said a voice. 'Look at that one! You'd better do something about him quickly or it will be too late.'

Mehrit sat up quickly, for they were prising Tekla away from her and he was whimpering. Two foreign ladies were looking down at him and saying something in a strange language. One of their own people, who knew French, was interpreting.

'This child must come at once,' he said. 'Where is his mother and the rest of your family? You must all come.'

'My father and mother have been taken south,' said Mehrit, 'and my grandparents are dead. There is only Tekla and me and my Uncle Gabre.'

'Then come,' said the young orderly. He picked up Tekla in his arms and walked away with the foreign ladies, and Mehrit followed as fast as she could. She was rather scared of these pale-faced foreigners with their strange language and she preferred the rest camps along the road, where her own people had cared for them. But she was not really anxious, for she had seen deep compassion and concern in their faces and she knew that they would do their best. They seemed to go on for ever, past those endless shelters where men, women and children lay, rested or queued for something or other. These travellers did not talk much because they had mostly come by the same route and now it was over, and there was nothing left to talk about. But at last Mehrit caught up with Tekla in a sort of Centre where the foreign ladies were doing very strange things to him. The orderly had put him in a basket and hung it on a hook and the ladies were looking on and approving, in spite of the little boy's miserable wailing. When Mehrit tried to rescue him, she was gently restrained and had to watch while they laid him on a board and measured him, like a piece of cloth.

'Give him to me!' she cried. 'He is frightened. What are you doing to him?'

The orderly quietened her. 'Don't be afraid,' he said. 'They are weighing and measuring him. He is sick; they will give him extra food.'

They were off again to another big shelter where the air was cooler and darker. There were rush mats on the ground and no crowds, only family groups with a mother or father in the middle, holding a baby or little child who looked exactly like Tekla; the same dull, sunken eyes, bloated stomachs and stick-like arms and legs. Another foreign lady greeted them and signed to Mehrit to sit down on an unoccupied mat. The orderly brought her two mugs of milk, some biscuits, and a bowl and spoon.

'Drink,' he said, 'and feed your brother. Break up the biscuits in the milk and give him a little at a time. And eat yourself.'

As Tekla lay in her arms, sucking in spoonfuls of milk and biscuit pulp, Mehrit wondered drowsily whether they had reached paradise. Spears of sunlight filtered through the rush mat roof, and over in the corner there was some activity where great cauldrons of high-protein milk were being prepared. But all around her were the rest of those who had reached the end of the journey. Even the children, grouped round a sick brother or sister, sat quiet and patient with a far-away look in their eyes, for they were mostly too weak to want to play and outside it was growing hotter and hotter. As the day wore on, whole families lay down to sleep together and Mehrit and Tekla did the same. And as she drifted off into dreams, she seemed to hear Tekla's feeble voice calling to her across the desert, 'We're not going to walk any more ever again.'

9

Tesfai stumbled on through the bush. He had lost track of time and was only conscious of the sun, blazing behind him in the morning and blazing ahead of him in the afternoon. When it scorched above him he lost his bearings, spread his wife's cloak over the brushwood and lay down in the shade. At night, he struggled on toward the warm glow that lingered in the sky long after sunset and then he lay down again. But some nights sleep was difficult because, in spite of the hot weather, he shivered so, sometimes burning and sometimes icy cold.

'I have caught the mosquito fever,' he said to himself. 'I cannot go much further.'

But thirst drove him on for, in spite of his care, he had nearly finished the contents of his water bottle and what was left was warm and brackish. His food was all gone but he had found edible leaves and roots and he had eaten locusts and cicadas. And now, the fever prevented him from feeling hungry.

He could not remember how long he had been following the sun in the west. He thought it was probably about the third evening when he lay down and drank the last drops of water. He was too confused to worry much and soon fell into a troubled sleep, broken by strange dreams and nightmares. He seemed to be standing on a long road, pulled in two directions; the misty figure of his dead wife pulling him backward and the living figures of his children pulling him forward. He awoke, sweating profusely, and he knew that he had slept much later than usual because the sun had risen behind him and was already flooding the morning landscape. He did not want to open his eyes and look. He had looked too long on scrub and thorn and stony hillocks and, apart from his thirst, he would gladly have turned back on that long road, lain down beside Muna and never opened his eyes again.

But he did open them and for a long time he did not move, for surely he was dreaming again. Also, fever played tricks with people's minds, and he refused to believe what he saw. But the sun, already hot, shone on his back and that was real. His lips were parched and his body damp and heavy with the sweat of his swinging temperature, and that was real. But could that collection of little clay homesteads, surrounded by small patches of green be real? He thought it must be a mirage of his tired brain, together with the shining strip of water beyond and the forest trees on the farther side. But as he lay gazing stupidly, unwilling to move in case the beautiful fantasy should dissolve, a woman came out of one of the houses with a pot on her shoulder and went down to the river.

There was no mistaking the reality of the woman. He struggled to his feet and stumbled toward this first sign of life he had seen in four days. He called out to the woman, pleading for water but she turned, frightened, and ran back into the house. A moment later her husband appeared in the doorway, carrying a hoe.

'Where do you come from and who are you?' he asked, and his eyes were full of suspicion.

Tesfai stood silent. If this was a government outpost, then his flight was over and he would soon be back in the camp to face criminal charges and a probable death sentence. People had also talked of bandits who roamed the bush; this man seemed unarmed, but that hoe in his hand could prove a formidable weapon. Then it seemed that fate took over; he had woken feeling cold and sick and suddenly he started to shiver. His teeth chattered, his head reeled. He fell on the ground in a heap, conscious of nothing but his longing for warmth and water.

The woman ran out with a little cry of compassion and knelt beside him. 'It is another of them,' she said. 'He has escaped from the camp and he has the mosquito fever.'

'I think you are right,' said her husband, prodding him gently with his foot. 'We will carry him under the tree in the shade and give him water. Later, he will talk.'

Tesfai lay in the shade of a mango tree all day as the fever soared again and seemed to be burning him up. But it was a good day because there was water in abundance, safety and kind human companionship. Every member of the little colony came and stared at him. One lad of about 8 years old appointed himself guardian and sat beside him all day long, fanning away the flies and holding a gourd of water to his lips. They brought him food too, *injera* and lentils and mango fruit. He ate and drank ravenously, and by evening the fever had subsided and he knew he would sleep well that night. He lay very still, his whole body bathed in the coolness that came at sunset, watching the crimson reflected in the still waters of the river and the small drifts of smoke rising from the cooking fires. Then, in the twilight, the man who had first seen him came and sat beside him.

'You have not far to go,' he said abruptly. 'You are only a little way from the border. If you start early tomorrow, you will cross before tomorrow night. There you will be safe.'

'Safe?' questioned Tesfai. It seemed a strange word to use. 'Is there food and water over the border?'

The man shrugged. 'Others have gone,' he said, 'and they have not returned. They say there is a camp quite close if you follow the sun and travel west. There is another one further north, but they say it is far away. There is water, many small tributaries of the great river. You are fortunate to have escaped. Two more came through yesterday. They say others died in the bush fire.'

Tesfai felt sorry. He would have liked to have travelled with those two and he wondered who they were. Who had lived and who had died? But they would probably have followed the sun in the direction of the westward camp and he must go

north, travelling toward his living children. He
thanked the man for his hospitality and told him he
would leave early in the morning. But he sighed, for
after the camp and the bush, it seemed like leaving
paradise.

'This looks like a new village,' he said. 'Have you
lived here long?'

The man scowled.

'We are the displaced people,' he said angrily.
'They took our homes and land for the rebels they
bring in trucks and planes from the north. We go
where we can and we plant as we may, but we are far
from others of our tribe, and the bush soil is stony.
Also, the river tributary is shallow and may well dry
up in the great heat. Then we too will have to cross
the border.'

'Do many pass through?'

'Some; there are other camps beside the one from
which you fled, but not many escape. Many try, but
some are shot down, and some lose their way and die
of hunger or thirst or heatstroke or snake bite in the
bush. Some are recaptured. But they still try!'

Tesfai smiled. He felt stronger and the fever
seemed to have left him. 'Those are they who, like
myself, have left children at home,' he said quietly.
'They draw you on. While they may live, you must
travel toward them. My wife died in the bush but she
told me to go on.'

'And what if they too have perished?'

Tesfai shrugged. 'Then let me perish too. What is there left to live for? But let me at least perish among my own people.'

There seemed no more to say. It had all been said long ago and the future was a grey mist. The man went to his hut and came back with a tattered blanket which he laid over his guest and told him to sleep. Tesfai was left staring across the shallow river which must dry up soon, to the fringe of trees beyond, black against the west. He would sleep for a time and then rise up and travel straight ahead by moonlight, guided by the setting stars. He must lose no time, for tomorrow the fever would return and he would have to rest.

But not for long, for he was not far from the border; he must travel north, and further north, following the great river. One day he would turn east and cross the border again – the merciful rains would fall… the great mountains would storm the clouds… a veil of green would fall over the parched land… his children would come running to meet him. But only in sleep could one escape like that from the chains of reason and common sense; for this was a dream.

10

Mehrit and Tekla settled down at the great border camp where every day seemed alike except that the April weather grew hotter and hotter and the flimsy shelter where they lived, next to the kind old priest, became more and more tumbledown. Tekla spent much of the day in the therapeutic feeding centre and had put on weight, but he was still dull and fretful and seemed too tired to run about. Early in the morning or late in the afternoon, when the shadows of the palm trees grew longer, they would roam along the dry riverbed in search of firewood and cook their *injera*. During the morning, Mehrit would queue up for water, brought in on the great water carts. Her once eager, active mind, now dulled with grief and boredom, refused to look into the future. It was enough that today she and Tekla were together, there was food and water, and she could lie down in the shade and rest. Gabre was a busy orderly now, but he visited them every day and the priest's old wife was kind to them. It was enough. One day Mehrit would look into the empty void ahead, but not yet.

She woke very early one morning because the child in the next shelter was crying, a hoarse wailing cry, and its mother could not soothe it. A small mist rose from the river and it was still cool. Mehrit lay still for a time, then she went over to where the woman sat, rocking her fretful little son.

'Is he ill?' asked Mehrit.

'I think so,' replied the woman. 'His skin is hot and his eyes are red and running with tears. I give him water but he cannot swallow. I think his throat is sore.'

'You must take him to the Centre. The nurse will see him.'

'Maybe; but there are so many and it is so hot. Here, under the trees, it is a little cooler. If I rock him in my arms for a time he will sleep.' Tekla woke up and trotted across to his sister, groggy with sleep. He climbed into Mehrit's lap and peered at his sick friend. 'Is Kiros ill?' he asked plaintively. 'Can't he play with me today?' He put out his hand and stroked Kiros' head. It had not been shaved, like most of them, but his hair was red and patchy from hunger. They sat quietly together for a time, but the wailing did not cease and Kiros would not drink.

'I will take him to the Centre,' said his mother at last, and she went away along the riverbank into the glare of morning. But she soon came back and her eyes were frightened.

'There seem to be hundreds of them,' she said, 'and they all have red, weeping eyes and running noses and they are all burning hot. Some are covered with a red rash. It will be near noonday when my turn comes. I will sit in the shade and go later. It is some sickness that has broken out among our children. You had better take Tekla away from here.'

Down at the Centre, a woman called Marie and her companions from the Swiss Red Cross worked doggedly on, fighting the measles epidemic. It had broken out in a matter of a few days and it spread like wildfire, racking those small emaciated bodies, bodies too ravaged with hunger to withstand the further onslaught of fever. They died like flies from the complications of measles, from meningitis, from mastoid infection, from diarrhoea and vomiting and dehydration because there were not enough hands to pass the gastric tubes and supervise all the feeding. There was seldom a time when, in some part of the camp, no sound of quiet wailing could be heard. The processions carrying those small, pathetic bundles on home-made stretchers became commonplace and passed almost unnoticed. The mounds in the burial fields stretched away to the burning horizon, row upon row. The temperature soared and the river sunk lower and lower.

Kiros died soon after the onset of the illness. He got his turn at the Centre and they did what they could, but he had only recently arrived and the journey from the cooler hills had taken its toll. On the third evening his wailing ceased. He lay in his mother's arms breathing rapidly, opening his parched lips for water but dribbling it out again. She would not take him back to the Centre for it was cooler under the trees and all she could give him now was quiet and the clasp of her arms. The sun was high in the sky next morning when he gave a little sigh, turned toward her and gave up the struggle. She called to Mehrit.

'I think he has gone,' she said. 'You had better call my husband and the priest.' She rocked to and fro, wailing and moaning for Kiros, her only son.

Mehrit joined in the wailing and the prayers but she would not let Tekla come near. Yet on that first morning he had leaned over Kiros and touched him and her heart was heavy with fear. She watched him all day and woke in the night to feel his forehead. But it was ten days before he crept into her lap complaining of a headache and sore eyes, and her body turned cold with dread for this was the beginning.

But the children had by now been inoculated and Tekla put up a brave fight. They had been several weeks in the camp and he had grown stronger to resist. As the hoarse whimpering started Mehrit forced the water down his throat and bathed his burning little body with her own ration. She carried him to the Centre in the cool of the morning and they gave him medicine and treated his eyes. On the fourth day the nightmare receded and she thought that he was going to live; only then did she dare to think about what might have been, and to contemplate the future without him.

He had sweated profusely in the night and his temperature had fallen. The hoarse crying had ceased and he lay in her arms, weak and ailing, but peacefully asleep. And because she had so nearly lost him and he had been given back, she looked steadily into the future and realised that their future lay together. She did not know how long they would stay in this scorching day to day existence or what change could possibly come, but Tekla would still hold her hand and lie beside her at night. Her life still had an object and one day the hot season would pass... one day Tekla would grow strong and beautiful... one day the rain would fall and the crops would spring up and they would go back over the border, he and she together. She would be older then. Her thoughts became hazy and indistinct at this point, for there were no parents or grandparents to go back to. Then, because she was nearly asleep, worn out with her nights of vigil, she seemed to hear Fikre's voice: 'Only a few months, and I will come and look for you. The rain will have fallen.'

She laid Tekla down on the burnous and stretched out beside him... Fikre was coming, running over flower-covered mountains, through harvest fields, to find her. She was young and she was beautiful and she was wearing her bright, embroidered dress; and the green, shining landscape smelt of rain.

11

Tesfai came upon other little settlements as he plodded on through the bush. They told him to follow the river, which came from the north-west and crossed the border not so far away. With adequate water his fever abated, and the river dwellers were kind and gave him food. As he journeyed, he met up with others and by the time they actually crossed over, he felt much stronger.

Most of the travellers were escapees from the resettlement camps, worn out with the heat and hazards of the journey and sick with hunger. When they had rested at the border they were glad to go on to the camp that lay westward, where they could once again rest and find food and water. But Tesfai did not join them, for some impulse of his own seemed to be drawing him north, although the way to shelter was far longer and the road lay partly through desert. He hesitated, fell behind, and sat resting at a diesel station by the side of the rough road that led north.

And then it happened; a truck that had been carrying supplies south and was returning empty drew up with an ominous rattle and a white man leaped out; at least, he should have been white, but his face and blond hair were covered with dust and his eyes were bloodshot. He opened the bonnet and peered inside, swearing softly to himself. Then he straightened and put his hand to his head. Both he and his truck were clearly in a bad way.

'Mechanic?' he asked rather desperately of the sleepy individual at the diesel pump.

The attendant shook his head and the white man, who was little more than a boy, swore again. Tesfai, who had been through high school, stepped forward. 'I am a mechanic,' he said quietly. 'May I help you?'

'You sure can!' exclaimed the boy. 'Have a look in here, then, and see what's wrong. The tools are on the seat. I'm shattered. I'm going inside to get a drink and a rest.' He stepped aside and was suddenly very sick.

Tesfai knew a lot about trucks. He had driven food supplies up from the capital and had worked for years as a motor mechanic. He felt his fingers come alive as they probed around and located the cause of the trouble. It was a small matter and he righted it quite quickly. When he went inside, the boy was sitting with his head on his arms, fast asleep with two empty Coke bottles beside him. Tesfai sat down too and wished that he could also afford a Coke. He did not wake the boy; after all, there was no hurry.

They might have stayed there all night had a quarrel not broken out between the diesel attendant and a passer-by. The loud argument woke the boy. He lifted his head and stared round him as though lost, until his eyes focused on Tesfai.

'Where are we?' he asked.

The boy looked ill and Tesfai tried to comfort him.

'Your truck is good,' he said gently, 'but the day is still hot. Rest more. Later, you travel on.'

The boy stared at him in amazement.

'No, can't do that,' he said. 'I've got to get back by tomorrow evening. But I feel terrible. I think it's a touch of the sun and I'm afraid of going to sleep at the wheel. I started out with a second driver but he suddenly took it into his head to go home. Well, I suppose I'd better risk it. I'll have another Coke and get going. Have one with me, and then I'll try the truck.'

He was wide awake now and, as they drank, he contemplated the skeleton-thin man in front of him with the gentle, courteous speech, and the deep-set eyes that looked like dark pools of sorrow.

'What's your name?' he asked.

'Tesfai. And you?'

'Oh, I'm Charlie. Let's have a look at the truck.' He rose to his feet but the room seemed to swim round him and he sat down again rather suddenly. 'Don't know how I'm going to manage,' he said miserably. 'Look, Tesfai, you don't drive by any chance, do you?'

Tesfai smiled. 'I drive trucks often. I drive, you sleep.'

Charlie looked doubtful. 'No licence, I suppose?'

'No, no licence. I am refugee. But I drive good.'

'Well, you'd better drive good. Let's see how you do.'

Tesfai climbed into the driver's seat. At first he thought he was too weak to manipulate the gears but as the engine came to life, he seemed to find strength welling up inside him from some unsuspected source. He thought that perhaps it came from the Coke, which was the best thing he had ever tasted. Charlie watched him, open-mouthed.

'Great!' he exclaimed. 'Right, just drive on. There are no turnings and I'm going to have a sleep. Thank God I met you, Tesfai!'

He closed his eyes and Tesfai smiled. 'Thank God!' the boy had said. Tesfai had forgotten that God was good and worthy of thanks and praise. This boy had reminded him. He was no doubt a very religious boy to remember God and for the first time in many weeks, Tesfai murmured a prayer of thanksgiving. God had helped him and Tesfai was travelling due north.

He drove for some hours through the burning, late afternoon and on into the kind coolness of evening. They passed through small, dusty villages and the river was never very far away. To his left, the sun went down and the sky flushed orange and scarlet and purple in the amazing nightly pageant, but Charlie still slept. At the next small settlement, Tesfai pulled up and prodded him.

'What's up? Let's go on,' mumbled the boy. 'You're doing fine.'

'I cannot go on,' said Tesfai gently. 'For a long time I have no food. I am a weak man. I must sleep.'

Charlie jerked himself awake. The cool dusk was healing and he felt much better. 'Oh, I'm sorry. It never struck me you'd had nothing to eat. Have a

sandwich, and we can get some more Coke here. I'll
bring you a bottle; or look, they're selling hard-boiled
eggs over there. How about one?'
Charlie's concern was overwhelming and he plied
Tesfai with strange European food out of a plastic
bag, food that he had never seen before and which he
feared would give him indigestion. In the end they
got out of the truck and sat under an awning and
Tesfai ate fresh bread and a hard-boiled egg and
drank Coke. He felt himself coming more and more
alive, partly through the food and partly through the
friendship and open admiration of the boy.

'You've been great,' said Charlie enthusiastically,
showing him a map. 'And I feel fine now. I'll take the
wheel for a bit and you lie down and sleep in the
back. Later on we'll change over again. Don't know
what I'd have done without you, Tesfai. You're the
best thing that ever happened to me.'

'It was God… thank God,' said Tesfai reverently,
gazing out into the deep blue dusk. He lay down on
a heap of sacks in the back of the truck. The small
night wind fanned his face and the moon rose over
the white sands of the desert. He remembered, for a
bleak moment, the mound in the bush where he had
buried Muna, but he resolutely turned his mind
away from it. He must look forward now. Charlie
was kind; God was good. He fell asleep to the sound
of the wheels rattling northward, northward.

12

Tekla did not die. His rash faded and the fever abated, leaving him thin and frail as a shadow, but ready to start again on the long climb to health and strength. But in spite of the extra food and care that a group of exhausted yet dedicated young workers could give to 75,000 needy people, the camp was no place to start that climb. The heat was increasing and the water supply sinking. The pools in the riverbed were nearly dry and the greenery on the banks had faded. Many of the flimsy shelters had fallen to pieces and there was nothing left with which to repair them.

Then suddenly the news circulated; they were opening another camp to the north and many would leave. Some were glad and some were sorry but there was little time for speculation. That very afternoon 40 open trucks were parked on the west of the riverbed, and families numbering 1,600 people were told to pack their belongings and be ready to leave at sunset.

Thousands thronged to wave them goodbye and to watch them mount the trucks. They huddled rather pathetically, clutching their babies, their bundles of clothing, their plastic water bottles and cooking pots. But the children were excited for it was an adventure to be riding north through the night and it might always be better further on. They shouted and cheered as the trucks rolled off into the dusk, and the crowds on the riverbank went quietly back to their shelters, wondering.

Almost every night the trucks arrived and those selected would pack up and go without protest. Mehrit waited with the others, for waiting had become a way of life and there was nothing else to do once she had fetched the water and baked the *injera*. She sat in the shade nursing or amusing a floppy little Tekla, and waited in hope for the coolness of the evening. They slept early, exhausted by the heat, and woke early, waiting in dread for the sun to rise. Even her uncle Gabre no longer visited them, for he had been taken off a week before the first convoy left to work as an orderly in the new camp.

Then one morning the summons came. Mehrit and Tekla and all those in their area of shelters were to be ready to leave by sunset. On the whole, she was glad. They would not be travelling alone. The priest and his wife and Kiros' parents would be coming with them and maybe they could stay together in the new camp. She left Tekla under a tree and went to collect her rations of sorghum and beans and oil. Then she made a bundle of their clothing and food and sat down to wait again. They slept through the afternoon and, when the shadows of the trees grew longer, she tied the bundle, the goatskin, the cooking pot and utensils on her back, took Tekla by the hand and they all started off together, the priest's old wife mumbling and crying a little because, having reached the end of her journey, she had settled down quite contentedly to wait for death in the shade, and she had not wished to be disturbed.

The trucks stood waiting and they climbed aboard, lifting the children and helping the old. There were 40 of them to a vehicle and no room to lie down, but most could sit and no one complained. Once again, the children laughed and waved but the adults sat quietly, their faces stamped with the age-old patience of the refugee, who waits with dull acceptance for the winds of fate to blow him where they will.

It was almost night when the gears ground and the trucks shuddered onto the road, one behind the other. The men and the children crowded to the parapet to wave a last goodbye and then they were off, westward toward the crimson streaks in the darkening sky. Everyone fell silent, because the rattling of the wheels and the jolting on the rough desert roads made conversation impossible.

The children soon fell asleep and the rest clung to each other and dozed as they might. The noisy, bone-shaking hours passed somehow and, at about three in the morning, the convoy halted by some long sheds. The passengers were given food and water and allowed to dismount and stretch their cramped legs. It was bright moonlight by now, the air was fresh and the orderlies were kind. 'Only another two hours,' they said, 'and you will arrive at the camp.'

The trucks had turned north-east and the tired travellers watched the morning steal in over the vast desert expanses around them – great stretches of dry earth, broken only by stunted bushes or the

shrivelling carcase of a camel or cow. There were no
shady trees here and even the road had given way to
a desert track. But the fear that gripped them
lessened as they came into sight of a line of trees,
clear against the morning. Many stood up and leaned
on the parapet to watch, for there was a green haze
over the land. There were clusters of small gardens
and a low, grassy area where sheep and goats grazed
among streams. Then they saw the great dam and the
gleaming reservoir and some let out a cheer; for
surely here, in this favoured spot, the water would
not fail.

They crossed the great dam and rattled on
eastwards across the desert again. The trucks were
speeding up now and almost everyone was standing,
shading their eyes, enjoying the life-giving breeze.
The camp loomed ahead of them, row upon row of
tents stretching, so it seemed, to a far horizon and,
right in the middle of them, lines of shelters – straw
matting fixed on poles – and people, endless people.
The trucks took a curve at a speed that sent them
flying into each others' arms and then drew up in
orderly formation in front of the shelters. They had
arrived.

People were running toward them: their own
people dressed in clean white shirts, and foreign girls
in cotton slacks and blouses; Mehrit realised they
were searching the trucks for the sick and the aged or
any who might need swift attention – she did not
know that it was not always possible to screen such
large numbers at the start, and sometimes only

speedy action could avert tragedy. Sometimes it was too late; a baby had been born in the truck one night and the young mother had died, arriving with her little family clinging to her dead body. There were frail children who had barely survived the jogging and jostling and they were hurried off to be cared for. The rest got down from the trucks and were escorted to a shelter where they settled down to wait. But the children, seeing the kindness, rushed to shake hands by the dozen, smiling up at their hostesses, their eyes shining in their thin, brave young faces.

They waited for a long time in the shelter. Mugs of milk and biscuits were served, and they were called in by families to be registered and examined, and the children weighed and measured. The white ladies seemed quite unable to pronounce their names or to understand what they said, but there were plenty of their own people to interpret. The long slow hours passed, the crowds grew thicker and the thermometer in the tent registered 120 degrees, but no one showed any impatience and no one became irritable. They had learned to wait. It was their way of life.

Tekla was weighed and measured but this time he was too tired to protest and hung passively on the hook. The nurse in charge consulted a brightly coloured chart, shook her head and said he must go to the feeding centre. Mehrit picked him up and was somehow pushed ahead, tripping over the bundles, stepping over the babies until they reached another shelter, darker, with matting round the walls and tiny pricks of sunlight piercing the rush roof and dappling the groups that sat below. It was all just as it had been before; the patient mothers, the starved little children, the cheerful bright orange mugs and the groups round the cauldron. Only one thing was different. A foreign girl sat with a baby in her arms and, alone among the brown rags and faded blankets, this baby was dressed in a rainbow coloured vest and was wrapped in a bright red and blue blanket, an amazing focus of colour in those drab, colourless surroundings. Mehrit watched, fascinated, while Tekla devoured porridge and lay down to sleep.

'Is it the child of rich noble parents, that they dress it like that?' she asked of the orderly who squatted close to them, feeding a baby with a nasal tube.

He smiled. 'Oh no,' he replied. 'It is a baby who arrived in the truck this morning. See, his mother is sitting near. Emma has dressed it like that to warm it because it was cold and dying. She is feeding it with a tube. It is too weak to swallow.'

They sat for some time. Mothers dozed beside sleeping children, pillowing their heads on their bundles. After two hours they would feed the children again and then they would go to their tents. Mehrit dozed, then woke and stared at the bright little figure and at the nurse who sat crooning over it, feeding it drop by drop.

Suddenly something happened. The baby gave a little gurgle. The nurse tensed and glanced at the woman sleeping beside her. Another foreign nurse came over and they both remained as though frozen, staring down. Neither spoke or seemed to breathe. They leaned over it together talking quietly. Then the second nurse pulled the tube from the baby's nose, took off its beautiful clothes and handed it back to its mother, who started to wail softly. The younger nurse turned away abruptly, the tears pouring down her cheeks.

'But why does she cry like that?' asked Mehrit, puzzled. 'Surely it must be her own child.'

The orderly, who was distributing milk, glanced across.

'No,' he answered, 'it is as I told you. It was a child who arrived in the truck this morning. It has just died.'

13

Tesfai slept soundly and woke only when the truck stopped in a noisy little market and Charlie poked his head round the back. 'How about some breakfast?' he said. 'Feeling better? If you can take the wheel now, I'll sleep.'

It was still early and they sat in the little café with the smell of blue smoke and frying all round them. Tesfai felt vaguely sick. While Charlie feasted on coffee and kebabs, he drank a bowl of broth and ate an orange. Charlie's eyes were red-rimmed and he kept yawning. He fell asleep over his last mouthful and Tesfai prodded him gently. 'You sleep, I drive,' he said. 'You lie in the back.'

'Not on your life,' said Charlie, jerking himself awake. 'You're a learner as far as I'm concerned! Until I get you a licence I'm sitting beside you. Let's go.'

They drove for five hours across a fawn-coloured landscape that should have been green and planted with sprouting harvests. Charlie leaned against the back of the seat and snored loudly while Tesfai went on and on along a road that seemed to rise up and hit him, glaring and dazzling in the heat. Sometimes he saw strange mirages of trees and water which disappeared as he approached, and he thought that his fever was returning for his head ached and his mouth felt like dry sand. It was noon when they reached a village near to a riverbank and he drew up in the shade of a palm tree and rested his head on the wheel. The jerking of the truck roused Charlie who woke and looked at his watch. 'Wow, it's midday and we've got as far as this!' he said. 'That's great, Tesfai! Let's eat.'

Somehow Tesfai managed to stagger to the little table under the awning and drink some ice-cold water. He tried another bowl of broth but had to go out in the middle of it and vomit. Charlie, who was stuffing himself with chicken and fried potatoes, came out and stood beside him, scratching his tousled head. He hadn't the slightest idea what to do, but he was sincerely sorry.

'Maybe you've caught my bug,' he said. 'I'm really sorry but it's only a 24-hour thing. I'm OK now. I'll drive, you get in the back.'

It had been dark for nearly two hours when they arrived at their destination: a crowded, smelly little drought town on the main road from the capital to the camps on the eastern border. Charlie drove straight to the hostel used by many of the famine relief workers in transit, regardless of their nationality, and told Tesfai to follow him. They went through a gate set in a high wall that surrounded a house with a well-kept garden. A veranda ran along the front of the house with rooms opening onto it but the rooms were mostly bare as the visitors had dragged their beds out into the open air where, as it was late, they were all asleep. But a tall dark-skinned man called Mengistu got up at once and offered to prepare food for them.

'Great!' said Charlie in a whisper. 'Anything that's going. We'll lift two more bedsteads out into the garden while you get it. Look, there's room down near the flower bed.'

Tesfai felt stronger and was able to enjoy a little salad and some lentils and, although he was too tired to talk, he knew that this tall, courteous countryman was watching him curiously. He was suddenly very conscious of his dirty clothes and grimy skin. It didn't really matter. Tomorrow they would put him in a refugee camp and it would all be over.

'I'm going for a shower,' said Charlie, scraping his plate. 'How about you, Tesfai? We're both pretty dusty. Let's change...' He broke off in confusion, realising that the man he had befriended had no luggage at all but a blanket, a cooking pot and a water bottle.

There was a moment's awkward silence, then Mengistu, who was clearing the plates, said quietly, 'You have come from far, maybe across the border. I can lend you a clean shirt for the night.'

'And I've got some spare trousers,' broke in Charlie. 'I'm a bit fatter than you, but you can tie them round. Come on, let's wash.'

It was good to be clean again. Charlie's soap and that blessed cold water seemed to wash away Tesfai's fever and headache and he lay down, cool and clear in his mind. The beds were close together; Charlie lay on one side, snoring already, and on the other, somewhat to his alarm, lay a blonde girl in a skimpy nightgown, fast asleep with her arms thrown above her head and her sheet turned down.

But he was too tired to feel embarrassed and anyhow, if this was Charlie's way of doing things, he'd go along with it, for he was beginning to like Charlie. He lay awake for a long time enjoying the feel of clean cotton, breathing in the faint scent of flowers in a watered garden, wondering about the future and thinking about the boy Charlie, who had not realised that you could not drive for ever on an empty stomach, who had plied him with food unsuitable for a semi-starving man, who had quite forgotten that he had nothing to change into, yet who had cared and lent him his trousers. Tomorrow, no doubt, they would say goodbye to each other. It would just be one more parting like all the others and, after all, there were plenty of refugee camps in this part of the world. He would be looked after.

He had travelled nearly four hundred miles north, and was not far from the place where he might one day cross the border back into his own province. He had been fed and clothed and treated with great kindness, and he should have been very thankful to God; but right then, he wasn't. In his weakness he turned his face to the mattress and wept.

14

When Tesfai awoke next morning, Charlie was perched on the end of his bed in a pair of blue cotton pyjamas, staring at him. To his relief, the girl had disappeared. Tesfai sat up and said good morning. Then he offered to wash his own clothes and restore Charlie's trousers but Charlie did not seem interested.

'Where are you going today, Tesfai?' he asked anxiously.

Tesfai thought about it. 'I came over the border from the settlement camp,' he said at last. 'My wife ran with me but she died in the bush... they shot her as she fled. My children were left behind when they took us. One day, when the rain falls and my people go back I will look for them. But today... I do not know. If you could take me to a camp I would be happy. I think I cannot walk any more.'

'Take you to a camp?' broke in Charlie. 'No way. I need a driver. I'm not going off on a long drive alone again, not after what happened this time. If I can get you some papers and a licence would you stop with me for a bit, Tesfai?'

Tesfai nodded gravely. Not for a moment would he betray the sudden lift of his heart. 'I am ready to serve you,' he said. 'But I must have clothes.'

'No problem,' said Charlie, suddenly slapping him rather painfully on the back. 'We'll soon settle that one.' He beamed all over his face and, to Tesfai, he looked absurdly young to be driving a truck at all. 'I'll have to get your papers fixed though and, as it's Sunday, that may take a day or two. Some of the offices may be shut. But in any case, you're not too fit yet, are you? And Mengistu says you can stay here and rest till I'm ready, so come and go as you please. I have to drive a food consignment to a camp up north on Wednesday morning. Not far, just a four-hour drive. I'd like you to come with me then.'

'On Wednesday morning you find me here,' said Tesfai simply, and Charlie bounced off, delighted.

Tesfai sat for a while enjoying the peace and greenness of the garden and the prospect of his immediate future, and then someone called him to breakfast. At first he was shy of joining this international group of young men and women, but their common language appeared to be English and they accepted him immediately as one of themselves. They seemed in good spirits but they ate and drank quickly for they had work to do, and he soon found himself alone with Mengistu. Tesfai helped him clear the table and wash the dishes and then Mengistu said, 'At ten o'clock I am going to worship God in our church. Would you like to come with me?'

Tesfai hesitated. There had been a time when, stumbling through the bush, he had not wanted to worship the God who had torn him from his children and taken Muna, but somehow during the last few days his feelings had changed. Charlie had reminded him that God was good and worthy of thanks, so he accepted the invitation. They set off at half past nine and walked past the mosque and the market and the basket weavers and the pottery stalls, till they turned down a side street and stopped in front of a long, low building. It was so quiet that Tesfai thought that they must have come too early. He was amazed to find, on entering, that the place was packed with silent worshippers who sat with bowed heads, and it was hard to find a seat. Children and young people sat on the floor or on the steps of the platform, and they were nearly all his own people.

And what a strange church! There were no icons or pictures or images on the walls, neither was there any smell of incense. The man who stood on the platform and gave out the number of a hymn was not dressed like a priest, and he spoke in Tesfai's own dialect. Then the singing broke out, bright and joyous with handclapping and there was a light in the faces of the congregation that he had never seen before. Then, strangest of all, the Bible was read in his own language and, to his further amazement, he noticed that many of the people had Bibles of their own and were turning the pages to follow. He listened carefully, for he had never read the Bible himself, and he heard, for the first time in a language he could truly understand, the story of the crucifixion.

At first it seemed just another cruel death to add to the many he had already witnessed, but as he listened his thinking changed. It suddenly seemed that there was no one in the room at all except that lonely man hanging on a wooden cross, representing all the lonely people who had died in the bush, by the wayside, of hunger and thirst, torture, disease and wounds. Had they all echoed those haunting words, 'My God, my God, why have you deserted me?'

Why? Why? Jesus had apparently not known the answer, or he would not have asked the question. Yet it somehow brought him nearer; not a plaster image or a remote historical figure, but someone who had come close and suffered as they had suffered. The service was closing and they were singing again, 'Oh how I love Jesus, he did so much for me', and their faces glowed as they sang. But why should they so love that broken, tortured figure? What exactly had he done for them?

He suddenly had a great desire to know more. The people were streaming out and the young man who had spoken from the front stood at the door shaking hands. When Tesfai's turn came he said shyly, 'Might I borrow a Bible? I have no money to buy one.'

The young pastor picked up a New Testament and handed it to him. 'Have you ever read it before?' he asked.

'Never in my own language,' replied Tesfai. 'In our church it is read in the old tongue that only the scholars can fully understand.'

He thanked the pastor and would have passed on, but found his hand held firmly.

'Would you like to come and talk to me at the church this afternoon?' asked the young man. 'I shall be here after the Sunday school, at four o'clock.'

'I will come,' replied Tesfai and went home with Mengistu to the midday meal. Charlie was paying his expenses until his papers could be fixed so he had nothing to worry about. He slept deeply after eating and when he woke it was time to leave.

The pastor, Isaak, was waiting for him in the church and it was cool and pleasant under the electric fan. They started by exchanging information about each other. Isaak had left his province, further south, two years previously, not because of famine but because of his faith. He had been 16 years old at the time of the revolution, but shortly after he had attended a small church and had been given a Bible. He had read about Jesus, the way to God and the Saviour of the world and, in a way that seemed strange to Tesfai, had fallen in love with him. He could not keep the glad news of Jesus to himself and had endured imprisonment, beatings and death threats because, not only would he not renounce his faith, but he had to tell others. In the end he was warned that he was to be arrested and shot next morning, and he ran away. Strong and athletic, he and his friend had crossed the border after running for 17 hours and landed up in a refugee camp. Isaak was well-educated and trustworthy and had soon found a job with the refugee organisations. He had built up the little church to its present fullness, drawing his congregation from the older, integrated refugee settlements. And every Sunday more new people crowded in.

'God has sent us famine, suffering and death,' said Tesfai, and his voice was bitter. 'I buried my wife in the bush. They shot her down as she ran; her feet were burned. My children were left alone, maybe to die. Why then should we so love this Jesus?'

Isaak was silent for a time, remembering the torture and the fear. Why had he loved so much? Why had life itself seemed almost insignificant compared with the joy of spreading that message?

'We live in a spoiled world,' said Isaak at last, speaking very slowly. 'God's way led to health and joy and love but we chose sin and selfishness and war; evil became our master and we became its slaves. But, spoiled and lost as we were, God still loved us. Your children are lost and far away, victims of an evil system, but you still love them and will travel any distance to find them. So God travelled a great distance to come to us. He became man; the man Jesus.'

'But what about the suffering, the starving thousands and the dead? What about the prisoners and those who die on the roads?'

'It is part of the evil and the spoiling that humans chose when they turned from God's laws to serve sin. You know, sometimes in our country, wicked bandits capture hostages and ask a great ransom. Jesus offered himself, his own perfect life, as a ransom to set us free from evil and bring us back to God. When he died on the cross he paid the price for the sickness and sin and suffering of all the world and all the ages. It is a mystery I cannot yet explain, but this I know: when we choose to bring our own personal sin or tragedy to the crucified Saviour, he bears it for us and gives us pardon, peace and triumph in its place. We can put it, by faith, into his hands. It comes in contact with his wounds and his love bathes it. Nothing totally committed to those hands can ultimately turn out evil. He will make something beautiful of it. But we have to choose.'

Isaak was speaking in Tesfai's dialect and he had never heard such words before. All the sorrow of the past months seemed to come flooding back over him and he wanted to weep. He was still very weak. He rose to go.

'I will read the book,' he said, 'and then I will understand more. I may stay here for a time as I have a job. I will come again.'

They said goodbye and he walked back to the house. There was an evening service at the church but he felt too tired to go, so he lay in the garden thinking about his children. He would get paid for his job and maybe he could save a little; if the rains came, surely some people would travel back. But would the children still be there? He found that his heart was beating fast and hard with love and longing and fear. 'You will travel any distance to find them,' Isaak had said. 'So God travelled a great distance to come to you.'

He opened his book and began to read about Jesus.

15

Mehrit and Tekla had settled down to their life in the smaller camp and, in spite of the scorching heat, they were generally happier. They missed the shade of the palm trees and the water holes in the riverbed but tents were easier to live in and more orderly than shelters, and the priest and his wife had allowed them to share their new home. Nearly every morning at dawn the number in the camp was swelled by the arrival of the lorries. But it never rose beyond 20,000 and, in the flatness of that drought desert, at least you could see where the camp started and where it ended.

Best of all, as far as Mehrit was concerned, there was Emma. Emma had brown curls, large brown eyes, a tilted nose and freckles; she worked in the therapeutic feeding centre, mixing milk and attending to the weakest babies. Mehrit had been drawn to her because she had wept over the brightly dressed baby, but she had loved her later that same day because Emma had loved Tekla. He had arrived, exhausted, from the night in the truck, looking like a tiny gargoyle and he had eaten and lain down to sleep. He had slept for so long that Emma grew alarmed and came over to look at him. She was only 23 and easily became nervous. She gave him a gentle shake and he woke and looked up at her, his ugly, bony face breaking into a big smile. For no apparent reason, he stretched out his arms to her and climbed into her lap and she sat on the floor and cuddled him until he was suddenly sick all down her front. But she did not seem to mind; she laughed, and sent Mehrit for another cup of milk. For Emma and Tekla, it was love at first sight.

Mehrit had known kindness all along the way. They had found Uncle Gabre, who now worked with the doctor, and he was kind in a grave, dutiful way. The priest's wife was kind too in a fussy sort of way, but Emma's kindness was different. There were dozens of little children in the Centre and she was kind to them all but, although probably no one else noticed, Mehrit knew that Tekla was special to her. Mehrit started to do small tasks for Emma, such as collecting the dirty mugs, or digging little holes, or mopping the rush mats when children with dysentery had failed to get outside the shelter in time. Most people thought that she was an orderly in training and, had it not been for Tekla, she might have been offered a job. As it was, she simply went on doing all she could for love of Emma.

Sometimes at noon, when mothers and babies mostly dozed, Emma would come and sit beside her on the mat and gather Tekla into her lap, and Mehrit would give her a language lesson. Mehrit had started to learn English at school and she knew a few words. It was wonderful to hear Emma say, 'Good morning,' and 'Drink your milk,' the right way in Mehrit's own language; or if she said it wrong, Emma would toss back her curls and laugh and then Mehrit would laugh too, and that was good, for it seemed a long, long time since she had laughed. Emma also taught Mehrit a few English phrases and that was good too, for it was months since she had learned anything except sorrow and patience.

Weeks passed and then, one day, there was a restlessness in the air, hot puffs of wind that lifted the tent flaps, a close, heavy atmosphere and massed clouds on the eastern horizon: the weather was changing. The occupants of the camp lifted their heads and thought about home; those in charge looked at the baked earth tracks and thought of truck wheels stuck in the mud.

All through the afternoon the wind rose until it was a tempest no one wanted to face. The mothers in the feeding centre had mostly gone to their tents but Mehrit still lingered. Tekla had put on weight but she herself was still weak and undernourished. She could not run fast through the storm with him and she looked round for help. Perhaps one of the orderlies would carry him.

It was Emma who came to the rescue. She appeared from the far end of the shelter carrying three empty meal sacks and put one over her own head and one over Mehrit's. Then she picked up Tekla, buried his face on her shoulder and covered him with the third sack. 'Now run!' she said, and they ran straight into the teeth of the storm, almost doubled up because the dust and grit blowing into their eyes was blinding. It stung their arms and legs and Mehrit led the way, choking and coughing, until they all fell through the door of the tent and collapsed, laughing. The priest, who had been mumbling his prayers, and his old wife, huddled fearfully in a corner, leaped to their feet in alarm. They could see nothing to laugh at in a storm that blew draughts of dust into the tent and they were shocked at such merriment. They scowled.

But it was difficult to scowl long at Emma. The Land Rover that would take her to her compound would not leave for another half-hour and she was enjoying herself. She could not talk to them, but she cradled Tekla in her arms and rocked to and fro, singing the songs sung to little children in her country. Mehrit, in her turn, sang the songs of her mountains and suddenly the priest's wife stopped scowling and joined in, clapping her hands and tapping her feet to the haunting rhythm. Then they all started clapping and tapping, often breaking down in laughter because Emma, however hard she tried, always got it wrong. It was a wonderful evening and, while Emma sat in the tent, they ceased to be afraid of the tempest outside. Even when she had to go, the memory remained like a beacon of hope. In spite of the dark months, they had been happy together. Laughter was not dead and the old songs had not vanished.

Emma covered her head with a sack and was almost carried back on the gale force of that stinging wind. But something had happened to her too. When she had come from England only a few weeks previously, she had been horrified by what she had seen. She had struggled with depression and homesickness ever since. But that half-hour in the tent had somehow been home: laughter, togetherness and love. Even that ragged old couple in the corner, clapping and swaying and enjoying themselves, could, basically, have been her own grandparents. She was beginning to learn that the outward layers can be very deceptive; you have to get down to the kernel, and the kernels are remarkably alike, the world over. Perhaps she need not feel such a stranger any longer.

Darkness fell early and they lay down to try and sleep in the windy darkness, but the storm blew harder and stronger and the dust and grit came whistling between the tent pegs, piling up beside them. They lay, half-stifled under blankets, wondering whether the tent would be lifted from over them, and waiting for a lull.

It came about midnight. The howling and whistling died away and there was a short, uneasy calm. Then, a quick patter of drops on the tent walls and the rain came down in torrents, churning the dry earth to mud, flooding the sanitation trenches, seeping under the tent flaps. Parents got up in the dark and sat on their damp meal sacks and blankets, holding their children in their arms, waiting, praying for morning.

For several days the mornings dawned clear and sparkling but each afternoon the rain fell in torrents, reducing the great plain to a sea of mud. One area flooded completely and all the tent-dwellers had to evacuate and move in with their already overcrowded neighbours. But the children loved it and no one could stop them playing in the polluted water, where filth and waste often floated like scum on the surface.

Mehrit and Tekla continued to splash through the puddles to the feeding centre every morning, but Mehrit knew that her days there were numbered; Tekla, although still a gaunt and bony 4-year-old, was improving fast and would soon no longer qualify for extra food. So she worked as hard as she could, trying to make herself indispensable to Emma, happy just to be near her and to sometimes meet her smile. Until one morning, when the rains were starting to clear, Emma suddenly ceased to smile. She arrived at the Centre ashen-faced and tense and hardly seemed to realise that Mehrit was there at all. Other workers came in from time to time and they talked in low voices, their faces grave and scared. When Mehrit asked Emma a question, she answered gently, but she did not smile. She looked as though she would never smile again.

Something was happening. For one thing, a shelter was being hastily constructed some way away from the tents and the Centre. It seemed as though almost every orderly in the camp was at work on it. Mehrit stood watching and wondering why they were in such a hurry; but even before it was finished, while it was still half-roofed, two still forms on stretchers were carried across to that new shelter. The girls standing with her looked at each other. 'It is a spreading sickness,' they whispered. 'They are taking them far away.'

Next morning, when Mehrit went to the feeding centre, Emma was not there, nor did she come all day. When Mehrit questioned the orderlies they said that Emma was working elsewhere. No one would tell her anything more, but rumours were rife and people were afraid. Day after day they huddled in frightened groups watching more and more figures on stretchers being carried into that ominous new shelter. Now and again, one was carried out to the far end of the burial ground, as though even the dead might be contaminated. Mehrit went about in a daze of grief, asking no more questions because she could not bear to hear the answers. For Emma had disappeared and so, surely Emma had the sickness. Perhaps she was already lying under some far heap of stones where no one was allowed to go.

Mehrit lay down one evening to sleep because she felt ill. It was still early and Tekla was grumbling beside her because he wanted her to take him out to play. But she took no notice, for her stomach seemed knotted up with cramp and she felt very cold. The priest's wife told her to get up and prepare the evening meal but she took no notice of her either. She turned on her side and drew up her knees and everything seemed so far away that she could no longer hear what anyone was saying and she did not care. Then she heard foreign voices above her but she could not understand their language. Somebody was kneeling beside her, examining her.

'Yes, it's another case of cholera.' Mehrit knew it was Peter, the young doctor, speaking. 'Fetch the stretcher and get her out of here as quickly as possible, and the bedding too. And that kid; take him somewhere else.'

Mehrit could hear Tekla howling as he was taken away and she felt herself being rolled on to a stretcher. After the darkness of the tent, the golden evening light hit her like a sword, but nothing mattered any more. Her whole body seemed to be turning inside out and she could do nothing about it. She was being jogged along and it seemed to go on for a long time. Then it was almost dark again and she knew that she was being laid down in the new shelter. Soon, no doubt, she would be carried out to the far end of the cemetery and Tekla would have no one. But she could not help it; she was too weak to do anything.

Someone was kneeling by her bed, putting a needle in her arm, moistening her lips, tending her, washing her. She didn't care. They could do what they liked. Then a voice said, 'Mehrit,' and she recognised that voice. With an immense effort, she opened her eyes.

Emma was beside her in a mask and white cap, but she would have known those brown eyes anywhere. She decided that, for Tekla's sake, she would live after all.

16

Tesfai got his papers and licence and became a full-time assistant to Charlie. They were both happy, sensing that deep comradeship that often develops between people of different races and backgrounds when they meet in adversity and share a common project. Tesfai loved Charlie for his young laughter and merriment which reassured him that, in a world of tragedy and disaster, some joy had survived. He also recognised his vulnerability. Charlie knew so little about the life and culture around him that if anything went wrong, he would not know what to do. Until it was possible to cross the border, Tesfai would stay with Charlie.

Charlie admired and respected Tesfai for his mechanical skill, but even more for his grave steadiness. Charlie could turn most things into a joke and wrote letters to his girlfriend that would have made her double up with laughter. But sometimes, especially at dawn or sunset, he knew that the jokes were like a curtain pulled tight across an empty space to hide the darkness. He held a responsible job and things were really bad – all those half-starved little kids, the fear that the food supplies would be held up, the anxiety about those desert roads when the rain came and, worse still, if the rain did not come... Charlie shook his head as he thought of all those millions in the west stuffing themselves and then going on diets. He just could not figure out what was wrong with the world. He guessed that jokes were his way of coping. But Tesfai did not laugh or make jokes. He did not even smile much because he had been right through tragedy and come out on the other side. Whatever happened, Tesfai would always know what to do. Charlie felt safe with old Tesfai.

So they unloaded and checked the stores and drove all over the countryside delivering food consignments to the various camps. And in this atmosphere of hard work, friendship and long quiet drives, Tesfai's strength returned and he was ready for the trials and hazards of the rainy season. Together they ploughed the trucks through seas of mud; sometimes foundering and having to lighten the load, or lay matting in front of the wheels, yet always managing to arrive, covered in mud, but in good spirits. But there were other days when travel on the earth roads was impossible and there was no work to be done. Then Tesfai took his New Testament and went round to Isaak on the chance that he too might be free.

He had read the book right through but turned back again and again to the life-transforming story of the resurrection. The opening words of Jesus to his disciples in the upper room had greatly moved him. 'Why are you so frightened? ... Look at my hands and my feet ...' He remembered Isaak's words. What had he said? Something like: 'What you commit into his hands comes in contact with his wounds. He bathes it with his love... he brings something beautiful out of it.' As far as Tesfai knew, he had committed his life, his children, his present and his future into those hands and had found peace. Because he had lost so much it was not hard to say in all simplicity, 'I, and all that I have, is yours.'

But he was beginning to realise that total commitment involved responsibility, loyalty and service, and in this area he was still groping. Isaak had shown him the verse, '... Christ did die for all of us. He died so we would no longer live for ourselves, but for the one who died and was raised to life for us.' But Tesfai still needed to work that out in detail. How could he live for his risen Lord in the shelter, in the truck, on the mud tracks and in his very limited conversations with Charlie? Prolonged sorrow and hunger seemed to have affected his memory and he had forgotten much of the English he had learned.

Isaak told him to live a day at a time. In the future, he might go back and tell the message to his own people. In the meantime, he could obey the commandments of Jesus, and seek to live the life of Jesus that he now realised had been given to him by the Holy Spirit. So he poured all his new-found love into his work and the care of the truck. Charlie, impressed with his faithfulness, selfless patience and rigorous punctuality felt vaguely, and rather uneasily, that he was living in the presence of a saint.

'It's weird,' he confided to a friend. 'If he'd just once get angry, get drunk, or have an affair or something I'd feel better. It's even rubbing off on me! I discovered the other day that I never swear when Tesfai's about.'

The days were lengthening to midsummer. The great rains that had fallen prematurely had held off for nearly a week and the sun and the wind were hardening the tracks. 'We've just heard that cholera has broken out in the middle camp,' said Charlie one morning. 'They need urgent medical supplies. We'll go after lunch, Tesfai, OK?'

'OK,' said Tesfai. 'I help you load.'

It was a bright windy afternoon and Charlie drove fast. Once on the desert track they slowed, for the soft earth made driving difficult, but Charlie enjoyed dodging the ruts and swerving round the puddles. When the tents came into sight, Charlie calmed down. He gazed at the great shelter, standing apart.

'I suppose that's where they're nursing them,' he said, 'and they say that some have died. We won't stay here longer than we need. Let's get to the store and unload.'

He drove along the back of the store and turned the corner faster than he should have done and then, in one second, it had happened. A small child suddenly ran out from behind a pile of cartons and disappeared under the truck. Charlie slammed on the brakes with all his might, jerking himself and Tesfai against the windscreen and an old woman screamed at the top of her voice. Charlie groaned 'Oh, no!' and his head sunk forward onto the wheel. He groaned again. 'Tesfai, Tesfai!'

Tesfai, feeling sick and faint, climbed out of the lorry and went down on his hands and knees, expecting to drag out a mangled little body. He peered under the engine and found himself looking into a startled, bony face and two dark eyes, sunk deep in their sockets. The child had not been hit. He had tripped and fallen exactly between the wheels and was now in the process of crawling out. Seeing a man's face close to his, the child stopped and stared.

Tesfai stared too. The bump on his forehead must have affected him badly for he was seeing things. He wasn't quite sane. He wished that old woman would stop shrieking for then, perhaps, he could get things straight. It was stupid to be lying in the mud staring when he should have been telling Charlie that all was well, but he just could not stop. He no longer seemed to be lying in the mud; he was back at home in the mountains and a tiny boy was running to meet him, smiling up at him with those same eyes.

'Tekla!' he whispered and pulled him out. He sat down by the side of the road and took the muddy, greasy little figure onto his lap. 'Tekla,' he said again. 'Where is Mehrit?'

'She's ill, they took her away,' said Tekla, but he spoke wonderingly. It was true that they had not been parted long, but it was long enough; and in that time, so much had happened. But now his memory was stirring…

They might have remained staring and wholly wrapped up in each other for a long time, had it not been for the yelling of the old woman, who seemed to think that Tekla belonged to her, and for an ashen-faced Charlie, who climbed out of the truck.

'Is he really OK?' he asked shakily.

Tesfai turned to him and now he really smiled – a big, ear-to-ear grin.

'This is my son,' he said. 'And he is very OK.'

**

It was a full fortnight later before Mehrit was allowed to leave the shelter. She had been very ill indeed and there had been a time when the nurse in charge had thought that she was slipping away. Now the worst was over, but she could not summon up the energy to start again. She had clung to life because she loved Tekla, and she still loved him but, at that moment, the very thought of him made her want to die with exhaustion. Then, as she lay motionless one afternoon, Emma came, her eyes shining and full of excitement, and told her, by interpretation, that her father had turned up.

Mehrit was very weak and her first reaction was to weep for her mother; but when the first storm of grief was over, it dawned on her slowly that she now had a father and the news could not have come at a better time. She lay, gazing through the doorway to the sun-kissed distances and blue sky and knew that she need never again shoulder the responsibility of Tekla – or the future. She could lay it down for ever and rest in the knowledge that all plans and all provision were now in Tesfai's hands. The great conflict of living was over and she relaxed in the peace of it. Her racing pulse slowed, her rapid breathing quietened and she slept.

'She's a lot better,' the nurse in charge told Emma. 'She's going to make it.'

Charlie was thrilled at what had happened and seemed to think that he had helped to bring this extraordinary meeting about. He found out the day of Mehrit's release from the shelter and organised a trip to the north camp. On the way there, he would drop Tesfai at the middle camp and pick him up again on his way home. He had even asked Tesfai whether he would prefer to go and live with his kids in the camp and had waited with bated breath for his answer. But, once Tesfai had worked out that by 'kids' Charlie did not mean baby goats, he had shaken his head. He preferred to work for his children and save up to take them home.

And so the great day came. Mehrit, looking like a living skeleton, was disinfected and released. But Emma had taken a personal interest in the reunion and had found her a blue dress from a parcel of old clothes and a blue hair ribbon that almost matched, and Mehrit sat on a rug, looking around her and feeling very beautiful. The scorching heat was over and, during her illness, the earth had responded to rain and the land was green, right to the horizon. Then she saw her father coming from the Centre with Tekla in his arms and she tried to get up to greet him, but found that she was too weak to rise.

They sat together for a long time: Tekla, happy and trustful, as though he and his father had never been parted; Mehrit, shy and a little withdrawn because neither was the person that the other had known previously. She had grown up, and he had aged, as though a lifetime of sorrow had been condensed into those five months. They would have to get to know each other all over again, but at least they made a start that afternoon.

'Father,' said Mehrit, 'when shall we go home?'

He sat considering. 'Not for this sowing, little daughter,' he replied. 'We are too late for a harvest and you are too weak to walk. We will not go back to the city. We will go to your grandfather's farm, in time to plough and sow before the lesser rains come. I believe that many, many will go with us: I will work and save to buy seed and an ox. We will rebuild what was broken down and plant the empty fields.'

Mehrit smiled. It was another six months before they would start, but she had learned to wait. 'I will come to the village and look for you,' Fikre had said, and she was sure that he would keep his word. He would be a teacher and together they would rebuild the scattered community. Of the enormous hazards of war, poverty and further drought she refused to think. This was the time for hoping and starting again. In any case, they were no longer her responsibility; she had a father.

She was too tired to talk for long and they sat in comfortable silence, enjoying the freshness and greenness round them, until Charlie returned. Tesfai also looked ahead in hope. He had been brought up on a farm; he knew the cycle of the seasons and the crops and he would learn the new sciences of irrigation and terracing from his own people in the rest camps. But he knew, too, that seed was scarce and an ox cost a fortune.

He knew that the war was not over and that the guerrillas in the mountains would not give in. The enemy planes would return over and over again, wiping out many a little village.

He knew that the rains might fail again at any season; that worm and pest might strike in any year.

He knew that the charity of the west was an uncertain commodity. Once a new sensation took the place of starving babies on their television screens, most of the giving would cease and the hungry would be forgotten.

But he had come home to his living children and he had found peace. They would live a day at a time, and he need not be crushed by the burden of the future. He too had a Father.

Nothing Else Matters

Lebanon in the 1980s and the country is racked by war. Lamia and her family are caught in the tensions as her brother is betrayed to the enemy by someone who was supposed to have been his friend. Lamia struggles with the hatred that threatens to destroy her, until she realises that forgiveness and love are the most important things.

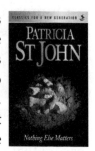

ISBN 978 1 84427 288 4   £4.99

The Victor

Evil hangs over Philo's family like a thick, dark cloud. His sister, Illyrica, is possessed by a power far greater than anything he knows. There seems to be no freedom from her curse and his mother is desperate to do anything to help her, even sell their boat to pay a magician to cure her.

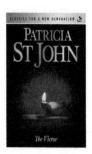

But rumours have come to the town about a prophet with amazing healing powers.

Who is he and can he help?

ISBN 978 1 84427 286 0   £4.99

These books are available from your local Christian bookshop, SU Mail Order (0845 07 06 006) or at www.scriptureunion.org.uk/shop